In An Empty Room

A Novel

Stephen Spotte

Published by Open Books

Copyright © 2018 by Stephen Spotte

Cover photo "Working hands" © by Janet Ramsden
Learn more about the photographer at flickr.com/
photos/ramsd/

ISBN-13: 978-1948598002

To the memory of Captain John Russell Warne,
U.S. Army, whose experiences in the Vietnam War
inspired this novel.

What if there's really nothing? Suppose I'm all there is?
What if there's only a child telling himself a story, and the
story is the child, and the child is me?

Denis Johnson, *Resuscitation of a Hanged Man*

PART ONE

Bunny

I listen to Poke describing how he trains Spooky using sugar cubes as rewards for behavior directed toward the goal he wants and withholding them when the behavior he looks for is misdirected. To the trainer that's called "positive reinforcement." Sometimes a reward is unnecessary when training animals, as when a dog enjoys chasing a ball. Then executing the behavior is its own reward and becomes self-reinforcing.

We humans are not different. What reminds us we're thirsty? We need water to carry out necessary functions like breathing, maintenance of vital organs, normal blood chemistry, and so forth. Being thirsty stimulates preoptic neurons in the brain's hypothalamus, which start firing and leads to tipping back the canteen. When thirst is quenched the activity of these neural cells tapers off, and we aren't thirsty anymore.

I learned this from listening to the LT. That's Marine grunt lingo for a lieutenant. Sometimes he gets on a riff about something scientific, but it's as if he's talking to himself and not even thinking about where we are or what we're doing or whether there's anyone around except himself. At such times he aims those empty-looking gray eyes at the distance, probably trying to imagine life in a clean white laboratory or wherever he was before the Marines. The veins of his temples stick up and throb like something important is happening deep underneath the bone. It might not be anything at all or it could be evidence of a serious event, maybe computations needed to predict the end of the world. He reminds me in some ways of the professors I had in college.

But I guaran-damn-tee you 'Nam isn't like any college, and the LT is no professor. We grunts speak among ourselves of comradeship, of the Corps as a brotherhood, and it makes us feel secure. Except the LT knows what most of us haven't thought about, that each of us is alone, especially in death. On patrol you hear him bark, "Okay, motherfuckers, why are you waiting around like visions in my nightmares? That includes you, Bunny, goddammit!" Then we stand tall and skid and slide down some muddy rainforest trail to nowhere.

You can touch the gloom, and the gloom touches you back. Pollen swirls like plankton in the narrow shafts of downwelling light adding to the sense of being submerged in a dark sea. Living silence shouts at you through every crevice, from the underside of every leaf. To city boys like me who never knew a true forest the highlands of I-Corps are a revelation: nearly impenetrable lianas thick as a man's leg clambering into the three-tiered canopy; in the low-lands the elephant grass with its toothy, vicious edges; everywhere biting insects and venomous snakes and booby traps. The whole place is its own war zone with conflicts occurring at different cadences measured by whether the conduits bearing life's fluids are phloem and xylem or veins and arteries. Everything is a battle over space: fungus against fungus, tree against tree, man against man. Lizards everywhere—on the leaves, tree trunks, rocks—harmless but ignored by Heaven. They're not godless life-forms, just irrelevant in Heaven's homocentric picture in which only those creatures serving humankind in some capacity matter. Everything else that creeps or scuttles or slithers with its belly on the ground falls outside God's terrible gaze. Or so it seems.

We might be in the bush a week or more, always on high alert, then suddenly coptered back to base for an interlude complete with cots, soap and showers, mail from home, hot food, and an honest-to-god fucking roof. The juxtaposition nearly drives some of the guys crazy.

What I'm saying is, you can learn a lot from the LT if you pay attention, provided you lean in close because he seldom raises his voice unless he really needs to jump on your shit. It isn't as if he's lecturing, but more like keeping his knowledge intact by reminding himself of what he knows. I'm sure he wonders whether he'll ever use it again if he makes it back to the World, which is more military lingo for the U. S. of A. Once I asked him what I now realize was a stupid question. We were on patrol and saddling up one morning when I said, "Sir, why keep moving? I mean, if there's no mission except to locate VC and radio in their locations and the VC are everywhere, why not stay in one place?"

He looked at me and said, "You studied science, Bunny. We move around hoping to demonstrate that every place isn't the same, to refute the null hypothesis of no difference between this piece of worthless, shitty ground and the next."

I know it's probably boring to hear me talk, but saying what I'm thinking out loud makes me feel better, takes the mind off the possibility of getting my ass shot off, lets peaceful memories surface and blot out the bad of the present, if only momentarily. Maybe it's the same with the LT. When I get to thinking it's usually about being at the botanical garden and seeing those amazing plants, reading the labels on them and learning stuff, then going home and closing the door to my room and turning over the information in my head, endlessly it seems. And so I tell this to Poke, who listens even though it's clear from the way he continues cleaning his weapon that he couldn't care less, but he hears me out because it's my turn to talk.

We have a polite relationship where Poke tells me about Spooky and when my turn comes I then tell him about studying plants, not only the studying itself but events related to it. He knows I spent hundreds of hours as a kid hanging out at the New York Botanical Garden in the Bronx. First he had to get over his astonishment that cities have places where people pay to go look at a bunch of plants that don't move or do anything except stand there stuck in the dirt, and that experts called botanists are paid good money to take care of them. When I first told him about botanical gardens he asked if even Houston had such a place, and when I replied probably he shook his head at the wonder and strangeness of everything. But when I get out of the Marines my goal is to work at the botanical garden as a botanist, one of the experts. How we earn a living carries weight. We ask strangers what they do for a living as a proxy for the dreaded question, who *are* you?

To Poke, plants fall into three categories. Trees have obvious value as timber and shade for free-ranging livestock, which any fool could see, and maybe as decoration at Christmas, the only time when somebody might bring a tree indoors. Other plants? Either they're useful as food for humans or livestock or they aren't. Seems pretty simple. When he thought a while Poke admitted there might be exceptions in this last group such as mesquite, which makes terrific firewood especially when camping on the range, and creosote bushes. He explains that some horses chew up the wood in their stalls. Nobody knows why, they just do. Maybe because some horses are ornery, which he pronounces as "*on*-ry." But if you paint the wood with creosote that behavior usually stops because horses hate the taste.

"Okay, so listen up," I say. Poke lifts his head a little to show his ears are working. "From our apartment on Washington Avenue in the Bronx I walk about five minutes to the bus stop at Webster Avenue and East 167th Street. I know the bus schedules by heart. I take the Bx41-SBS heading for Williamsbridge Gun Hill Road and get off at Webster Avenue and Bedford Park B1, the Mezzanine. The ride is twenty minutes, give or take. From there it's a halfmile walk to the botanical garden, which takes me maybe fifteen minutes. I have an annual pass, so I go through the members' entrance instead of standing in the ticket line with the tourists. All the guards and ticket takers know me. You could say I'm an anomaly, which means I look different or out of place. Who expects to see a black kid my size with an interest in plants you can't even smoke?"

After a few seconds Poke says, "I reckon so." That's typically the only feedback I ever get, but it's enough. I say what I need to, if only in company slightly less disinterested than the humid air, and somebody actually hears the words. In biology they teach you that speaking is the propagation of sound, and hearing is its subsequent reception. None of that counts in the end. That it happened is what matters. After saying my piece I feel myself relax, become aware of the tingling sensation of my nerves subsiding, sometimes even a miniscule rush of endorphins culminating in a transient high. I know Poke feels these same sensations when it's his turn to talk. I can tell by how he settles back with hands clasped behind his head, not quite so twitchy, sometimes a little wisp of a smile on his lips. What actually matters is we've just reinforced our common bond of humanity. Sort of like horse training, I suppose.

The LT

Anywhere is preferable to here. I need a place where silence could swell enough to absorb the distance, where I can laugh soundlessly and remain invisible; where the sky strains, cries out, and gives birth to ecstasy. Meanwhile I can't stop thinking about details, even when most are useless considering my location and responsibilities. In the end it's futile: whether you seek differences or sameness you arrive ultimately at the same place.

I've been leading a Marine fireteam on patrol here in the northern highlands of Vietnam near the DMZ for several days, with more scheduled before the mission is accomplished and we're evac'd back to base. We're located about as far north as possible and still be in the South. I've led my team on patrol at least a dozen other times since we've been based here, and we still haven't engaged the enemy, probably a good thing considering none of the men except me has ever been in a firefight. I was in several during a first tour; this is my second. Exactly how many patrols we've been on at this location I couldn't say without consulting my notebook.

That's why I'm always amazed when some bit of esoterica, some element of a physiological process or sequence of numbers, has sudden relevance, especially out here where we live and die like primitive life-forms, brainless, at the mercy of equally brainless superior officers who decide our fate from a safe distance. I'm referring to the higher-highers sitting in their air-conditioned "war rooms" in Saigon studying maps and holding meetings to decide who among us is next to get shoveled through death's front door, then afterward kicking back sipping expensive bourbon and masticating medium-rare sirloins. War is social devolution. It reintroduces humans to elemental savagery, the status of each state's civilization distinguished only by the level of technology achieved to most efficiently slaughter its opponent. Hey, we have the atomic bomb and you don't. Is that cool? Better not fuck with us.

So it came as little surprise when I stopped with my men one steamy afternoon a few days ago to rest along a narrow trail and began thinking about the human sense of smell. We were on low alert and the men had been muttering softly to each other as we trudged along single-file. Behind me I heard Hillbilly say to someone, "Man, you really stink. I mean, you stink bad, worse than one of them water buffaloes." This brought a chuckle from the recipient, who I knew to be Bunny. Truth was, of course, we all stank. As I said, we had been in the field for days and looked ahead to several more. It was put one foot in front of the other and hope you didn't step on a mine or stumble over a trip wire linked to an IED.

Ever since the French anatomist Pierre Paul Broca concluded in the nineteenth century that humans have stunted olfactory perception scientists have accepted it as fact. Broca based his conjecture on the large size of the human brain and its comparatively small olfactory bulb, a tradeoff he attributed to humans having the gift of free will. The olfactory bulbs of other mammals are larger relative to brain size. Neurologists now know that Broca was wrong. Humans are actually terrific smellers, better in some situations than dogs and even rodents, animals considered near the top of the olfactory kingdom. Why is this relevant? It probably wasn't until Injun came along and showed me a way of perceiving the world I wouldn't have thought likely.

Odor detection, or smelling, is an intriguing sense. Some scientists have proposed that odors are detected and differentiated when groups of neurons in the olfactory bulb coruscate as "odor images" analogous to retinal images deployed in vision. Both forms of "images" are difficult to describe in words, perhaps indicative of a similar neurological origin.

Evidence that humans are inferior smellers presumed an anatomical basis: during evolution our faces gradually flattened, our snouts became shorter, and we began to walk upright, the implication of this last being that with our noses farther from the ground where many smells important to survival emanate, odor detection became less important than sight and hearing. Different changes were occurring simultaneously, like our eyes moving to the middle of the face and shifting closer together enhancing stereoscopic vision and depth perception. Sight and hearing became more important than smell, but this simple model discounts the importance of the rapidly enlarging human brain. In truth, humans can distinguish more than a trillion odors, an ability enhanced and augmented by our brain's capacity to sort and interpret olfactory information both in the present context and in memory.

We were coming up from a valley on a narrow trail nearly overgrown by head-high vegetation, aiming for an unnamed ridge. Poke was walking tail-end Charlie. He suddenly shouted, "Holy shit!" and squeezed off three rounds. The rest of the team hit the ground on either side of the path and turned in unison to face behind us. At ground level the vegetation obscured everything. "Stay down!" I whispered and rose slowly. From a few feet ahead an unfamiliar voice whispered back, "Don't shoot!" I dropped to a crouch and aimed my rifle toward the words, fingering the trigger. "Come out and show yourself," I said in a normal voice, then added for the benefit of the team, "Hold fire."

If I hadn't been prepared for the voice out of nowhere, I was even less prepared for the man who appeared suddenly in front of me. He was slight and scrawny, maybe half Bunny's weight, and tanned to a dark copper. He was all sinew and gristle, barefoot and nearly naked with a string of dog tags around his neck. I noticed only remnants of his original 782 gear: the oversized cut-offs of what were once rip-stop utility pants and a K-bar knife in a sheath dangling loosely from a makeshift belt cut from issue nylon rope. He was without the usual lensatic compass and either didn't need it or was hopelessly lost in the rainforest. Nor did he have a firearm or rucksack. He carried essentially nothing. His hair was shoulder-length, and what passed for a beard looked scraggly and sparse as if cultivating facial hair was not in his heritage. The irises of his eyes were as black as his hair.

"Identify yourself," I said.

"Private First Class Lanoka, Force Recon Company," he said, "But call me Injun. Everybody does."

Poke

When I joined up they called me Cowpoke. At first I didn't like it because I thought they was making fun of me, but eventually I figured out they wasn't. Then it become just Poke. Every grunt in the Corps (or the "Crotch," as we call it) seems to have a nickname, and mine could be a lot worse. In boot there was one kid they called Numbnuts, or just Nummie for short. He was always screwing up and then trying to cover by mouthing off. If you're paying attention you learn fast to keep your lip zipped and your head down and don't give shit to nobody, especially to a DI or you'll end up wearing it yourself sooner than later. If a DI tells you to polish that floor until he can see the reflection of a tiny little mole on his forehead, you polish hell out of it. So now I feel kind of proud because when someone yells, hey Poke, I know that's me. There's lots of Bills and Bobs around, but so far I'm the only Poke in this platoon.

I reckon the name fits, or at least Cowpoke does, because I'm from the borderlands of southeastern Texas. Scrub country. And I been around cattle and horses all my life. The Rio Grande practically flows through our backyard. Pa has a ranch of eight thousand acres a little west of the town of Los Ebanos, population maybe two hundred if anybody cares to count. We have a couple of milk cows, run some beefers, grow hay and a few vegetables mostly for our own use, and keep pigs and chickens. Since Ma died there's just Pa, my little sister Jimmi who's fifteen, and a Mex ranch hand named Jorge who lives in Ciudad Diaz Ordaz about four miles south of the border. Several thousand people live in Diaz Ordaz, which makes it lots bigger than Los Ebanos over on our side. Anyway that's pretty much our story. Ma foaled just the two of us kids if you don't count the one stillborn that come out of her dead as a stone. It come spaced between the two of us in birth order, me and Jimmi. Don't ask if it was male or female. I couldn't tell you; nobody ever said.

Los Ebanos is famous for its hand-pulled ferry that goes back and forth across the river. It's the last ferry of its kind along the whole length of the Rio Grande. The river is only about seventy yards wide near the crossing, even less during low water, and at places upstream and down where the sand has formed shifting bars and partly filled in the riverbed you can wade across and not even get your ass wet, or if you want to stay completely dry, ride a horse across and raise your stirrups some. On our side the ferry cable is anchored to a big old Texas ebony tree, and that's how the town got its name. The ferry can take twelve pedestrians and three vehicles per trip, and five men are needed to pull the rope, but if the crew is shorthanded the passengers fall in and tug on it too. A crossing takes only a few minutes. There is no schedule; the ferry runs on a as-need basis. Hell, I can't tell you how many times I helped pull that boat across, and I'm talking in both directions.

·

The LT

The facility with which men bond with an unfamiliar machine to the extent of staking their lives on it is a curious thing to watch. Some take to it readily, others indifferently, still others not at all and have to be coerced. To this last group the machine is alien, any supposed benefit suspiciously abstract. They recognize in a machine a certain utility, if vaguely, but loathe the cold hardness of its working parts. The mechanics of its movements are dismissed as disruptive noise, the same attributes one who bonds with machines finds soothing, even reassuring. The born bonders admire the solid click of gears and sprockets meshing cleanly, the odor of lubricants, the contented sounds any machine makes when functioning according to its design and cared for by loving, capable hands.

Depending on predilection, a field soldier or Marine becomes either a comfortable organic extension of his rifle or the rifle remains an uneasy inorganic extension of himself. Hillbilly has an off-hand relationship with his weapon based on having hunted since he was a small boy. Poke also had an

early familiarity with firearms, although his attach-
ment is unusually intense and personal. Bunny, who
grew up in the urban projects and knew of neighbors
killed by random gunfire, approached arms training
with considerable trepidation. His weapon is exclusively a tool; it could never be a friend or companion.

It's difficult for the warrior to accept that he's not just
mortal but also marginal. Lots of us of were marginal-
ized Americans, either conscripts or deluded volunteers.
Killing the enemy became easier after we stopped
thinking of them as human. We came to address meaning inside the context of form: we were wet because
of the rain, hot because of the sun, wounded or dead
because flesh is more tender than steel.

All wars are us against them, the sanctified and
blessed against the unholy and damned, the civilized
against the wogs and barbarians. We demonize our
enemy, making him less human than ourselves so
we can kill him without guilt. The M-16 rifle, our
standard issue weapon, is a mass-produced machine of
intricate parts. Its function is to fire bullets at human
beings whose ideologies differ from ours. These other
humans are America's enemies, which by default
makes them my enemies too. They're gooks, slopes,
slants, dinks, not like most of us. Their speech and
culture are Asian, not American, and their uniforms
are different. Although we don't know these people
personally it's our duty as American military personnel to maim and kill them whenever possible with
the objective of reducing their numbers until they

relinquish their culture and ideologies and accept ours as superior.

The M-16 has been designed as a portable killing machine. Fully assembled it comprises numerous separate and tightly integrated parts, but its design is such that after extensive training and practice a soldier or Marine in the field can quickly take apart, clean, lubricate, and reassemble the comparatively few components necessary to maintain it in working order. Some individuals learn to start and complete the maneuver even at night or while blindfolded, and often take deserved pride in their accomplishment.

They tell you during training that in a "weaponized situation" a clean, well-functioning rifle can save your life by not jamming at a critical instant when you need to return fire. Time permitting, you are encouraged to field-strip your weapon and clean and lubricate its components daily, if possible. Only then will it remain in good working order. After you and your weapon have spent hours wallowing in rain and mud, wading across streams, or humping together through miles of red dust, an M-16 needs loving attention even if it hasn't been fired.

When stopping to sit down and rest, take off your boonie cover and place it upside-down between the thighs of your crossed legs and only then start to field-strip your rifle. Treat the hat as a bowl and put all the little parts inside it. Some of the pins are quite small. Always carry spares in case you lose one. Lose a pin in the mud or vegetation without a replacement available and you're fucked, plain as that. Fucked. Think of a weapon as a car, then think of you, the driver, standing beside a lonely country road out of gas and feeling stupid. Except that in the present situation someone might be shooting at you, and you have no means of defending yourself.

Your weapon can nearly always stand a full cleaning, but time is often short until you're back at base. Either that or you're beat after patrol and just want to flake out, if only in a fighting hole half-filled with muddy water. Most guys give their weapons a fast clean when in the field. We could have worked through the sequence in our sleep and oftentimes nearly did. Drop the magazine, clear the chamber, click on the safety (remember the mantra, safety first and last). Pop out the rear pin, shotgun the upper receiver open, pull back the charging handle (but don't remove it) so the bolt-carrier group slides out. With your nylon brush take a quick swipe at the chamber area and the bolt face plus exposed extractor, and don't miss the grooves of the bolt carrier. Lost your cleaning brush? In a pinch a toothbrush makes a passable substitute. A Marine gets used to the bristles tasting of combusted carbon and CLP. Like a condiment, right? Then snap up the hammer. Suck wind and blow any carbon into the lower receiver group. Wipe the bolt-carrier group with a clean rag. Apply one drop of CLP between the bolt and carrier but keep it away from the bolt face. Apply a little CLP along the grooves of the bolt carrier, although spare the forward-assist grooves. Pull back the hammer and reassemble. Remember the mantra, safety first and last. Work the bolt carrier a couple of times to spread the thin coating of CLP evenly. Hope to hell everything works in sync when you need it to.

Bunny

Poke is one of those dudes who establishes an immediate affinity with anything metal that has moving parts. Of course his first love is horses, and one horse in particular, Spooky. The rest of the guys send money home to their families; Poke sends it to his horse in care of Jimmi. A horse obviously can't use money, but it needs special vitamins and stuff, and when she receives the pay order his little sister spends the money on that.

After his horse, Poke probably loves his rifle next best. He enjoys breaking it down and cleaning each little item, each pin and moving part and applying CLP to keep everything lubricated and rust-proof and functioning smoothly; as the saying goes, like a well-oiled machine. I can tell doing it makes him happy by the secret little smile he reserves mostly for this task, a look I rarely see at other times. I have to say, Poke really doesn't notice much. Vietnam seems to him a place of eager and abrupt vegetation and semi-feral dogs just slightly evolved above the rodent. There were many who would doubt he'd ever been anywhere, himself among them.

Sure wish I were as corrosion-proof as Poke's firing pin. I'll tell you what, all of us—the entire squad—might as well have joined the Navy instead of the Marines, considering we spend more time in water than most squids. If we're not half-drowned in a rainstorm or standing in our fighting holes balls-deep in muddy water there's always enough wetness to keep our boots soggy. Our feet haven't been dry in weeks. No wonder the microbiota find life good between our toes. An old sergeant I ran into told me he had been in the Second World War, then Korea, now here he was in 'Nam. He'd caught immersion foot in the South Pacific in that first go-around and it never did cure up. He figured he'd die with scaly feet, take the shit with him right into his coffin. "Fuck it," he said, "I ain't got the time to worry about no fucking jungle rot. Out here you cover your fucking ass first and later think about fucking covering your fucking feet."

About Poke's rifle, I swear he sleeps with his arms wrapped around it like it's a woman or maybe a teddy bear. No stacking his love-toy against a tree. He adores the damn thing and never lets it wander out of reach. The LT noticed this too and mentioned something that had never occurred to me. The LT knows lots about everything. I might recognize the plants better than he does, but the rest? No chance. He's an educated man, for sure. Don't know his educational background, but he must have more degrees than a thermometer, the stuff he can tell you. But he's quiet, not one to show off. He just mentions things, weird things, and leaves you standing there thinking about what he said. Not that most of us will ever understand completely.

The other day when he noticed Poke copping some sleep with his arms hugging that M-16, he mentioned to nobody in particular that our mistaken sense of the self—our first-person selves as individuals—is largely based on what he called "phenomenal owner-ship" of our bodies and minds. By "phenomenal" he meant as in the phenomena of sensory perception and interpretation of sensory input by the brain, not its other meaning of fantastic or extraordinary, although it's certainly that too. He was referring specifically to the mental phenomenon of Poke feeling owner-ship of his rifle the same as his arms and legs—as an extension of *him*.

The LT evidently studied neurology because he brings it up a lot; among other things, which parts of the brain interpret and convey specific functions. He mentioned that the "body schema" is an uncon-scious sort of computer program run by the brain that maintains and updates a map of our posture, the positions of our limbs, and so forth. In other words, it recognizes them as exclusively *ours*. When we learn to use a new tool the neural network is altered to incorporate the updated information, which is then integrated into the body schema and becomes a part of us, like an additional arm or leg, a finger or toe.

This is where the M-16 fits in. The military is dimly aware of the association, according to the LT, and capitalizes on it. All our training is based on this principle. We field-strip and reassemble a rifle so often it becomes part of our unconscious selves. We do it without thinking. Each of us integrates the sequence of maneuvers into his personal body schema until the rifle and its component parts become an extension of ourselves similar to another limb, all of it caused by this mental shift as our self-model is reconfigured in the parietal lobe of the brain.

At first, the LT said, men probably killed each other up close with their hands prior to inventing clubs, the use of which gained them a little physical space in battle: instead of being right in your opponent's face you were now a club-length away. Eventually weapons evolved into spears and later bows and arrows, allowing murder and mayhem at even greater distances. The rifle is just a more highly evolved tool than a spear or arrow: it extends the killing distance still farther by expanding its user's "behavioral space." With each step in the evolution of weapons the simultaneous expansion of behavioral space allowed killing to occur at increasingly greater distances while remaining extensions of us as part of the body schema.

That space continues to expand as weapons become more advanced. Think of aerial bombing, artillery shells that can travel many miles to the target, and ICBMs capable of spanning continents.

Natural disasters—volcanic eruptions, earthquakes, avalanches—being guiltless tragedies, are easier to tolerate than destruction caused by humans. This is because human behavior carries a moral charge inseparable from agency. Today you don't even have to see your enemy, much less murdering him while looking him in the eye. Unless you happen to be a bush Marine.

The LT

I've spent too much time surmising, too little con-
cluding. I don't exist, for example. What we call
the living world is imagined by the brain, which in
concert with sensory input creates what we think
is reality, or the world outside. Our phenomenalist
experience is this illusion. Where among the tangle
of neurons with their dendrites and synapses is the
"self?" Nowhere. There's no such entity, nothing
identifiable with assurance as *me*. Nor has there ever
been. I look down at my boots as I trudge along this
muddy path. I glance at my mud-spattered cammies,
listen to the squishy sound our collective steps make
in the mud and I think, who—or what—is the thing
undergoing this experience?

My neck itches from new mosquito bites layered
atop the old ones not yet healed. I recognize the
sensation as a manifestation of angry nerve endings.
Specific itch-processing neurons in the spinal cord
transmit signals to the parabranchial nucleus, a different cluster of neurons in the brain stem. Disrupt
this link and the urge is quelled. No more infected

sores scratched raw by dirty fingers. Gone along with itching is the complaining about bugs and their bites, about the stinging discomfort from sweat running into open sores. No more itch and bitch.

Conceptually, consciousness seems refractory to reductionism; it withdraws, leaving us alone and exposed to our egos and hubris. It jabs and feints when we try to grab and restrain it, to ask its identity, *to show itself*. Consciousness camouflages its protean manifestations, eluding and deluding so expertly— with such transparency—that we are lulled into believing we exist, that we blend inseparably with a mysterious "self." I catch a glimpse of the wraith that poses as my own consciousness—as the first-person "I"—vaguely aware of its role as the grinning trickster playing jokes on my senses, invisible inside clouds of endorphins and fooling me into false exis- tence. Everything seems so obvious. One must know himself, isn't that right? This absent self that seems ubiquitous will accompany me laughing into death, a mutual conflation because it will die at the same instant "I" do. But why should the illusion of my nonexistent self be concerned when illusions can't be real? Or perhaps they can be if viewed in the guise of real *false* illusions. And what about the so-called "I," my ego? Or this specific illusion's physical projection, a walking, pulsating sack of guts? Why should it care either? If the illusion is all-encompassing then so are discomfort and pain, guilt and sorrow and delight, the fear of dying so excruciating as to seem transcendent,

like a fleeting synesthesia arising from the foul odor
of a dream.

Poke

Me and Bunny must make a weird pair of buddies, him a big black city kid and me a scrawny white kid from south Texas. Who would of thought it. We ain't got a damn thing in common, but we like to talk anyway. Besides, there ain't much else to do when you're in the bush and hunkered down in a muddy fighting hole hoping the VC don't start shelling your ass or sneaking up on you from the perimeter. You sometimes wonder if the words you're whispering to your buddy will be the last you'll ever say, and when you think about things that way you don't want your last words to sound stupid.

I have one goal in life: I want to be the best, most bad-ass calf roper ever seen at the rodeo. Calf roping is the most intricate rodeo sport of all. Riding rough stock—broncs and bulls—might get you more applause because of the danger, but roping requires lots more skills. You not only need to throw the rope but you got to jump off the horse after you've lassoed the calf, toss the critter on its side, and tie up three of its legs quick as you can. And maybe most important, you need a good roping horse, one that's in sync with your every movement. In turn, you know your horse's every twitch and mannerism. Once that calf comes out of the chute there's no longer a man and his horse, just a "manhorse," I guess you could say. In some ways a roper and his horse is tighter than a marriage, surely tighter than any friendship you'll ever have. If you and the horse can't work as a unit you'll never be top gun at a rodeo.

Think of the situation like this rifle, which only works to my benefit if I keep it clean and oiled and know every little quirk and hesitation in its moving parts. Maybe that's where the term "rifleman" came from. Notice it's one word, or I think so. Got to remember to ask Bunny. I got to hand it to Bunny. He's smart. He graduated college, and I never finished high school. Shit, Bunny could of went to OCS. When I told him he said he never wanted to be no officer, that being a grunt is just fine. Less responsibility, he said.

I have a horse named Spooky back home. He's a stock horse, what's sometimes called a "cow pony." He's mostly quarter horse, and I'm planning to teach him roping. I bought him a couple of years back for eighty dollars from a stockman near Los Ebanos, a friend of Pa's. I borrowed the money from Pa and worked as a hand for him and other ranchers for two years to pay him back. I handed Pa the last ten-spot just as I boarded the bus for boot camp. Spooky was three years old when I got him and already used to herding cattle. I liked him for lots of reasons, one being his strides are short, which helps the rider to keep speed on his rope. He's five now, and he'll be nine when I muster out of the Corps. That might sound old, but the truth is most good roping horses don't come into their own until age thirteen or so and some well into their twenties. By then a roping horse should be completely broke, knowing all its own moves and the rider's too.

A top roping horse can go for ten thousand dollars, sometimes more, but only after years of training. Most horses flame out and never get there. Of course I'm just learning calf roping myself. When I get home I'll need to catch up on how to train Spooky, and I don't expect a easy time, especially with helping Pa work the ranch. For starters I'll need to buy a calf to practice on. When it gets too big I'll sell it and buy a younger one.

Bunny

I have to admit, hanging out with Poke has expanded my vocabulary, in addition to turning my attention to plants I'd never thought much about, grasses in particular. Poke only talks about horses and other livestock and how he wants to be a rodeo star roping calves. He'll be talking away, a dreamy look on his face, then say something like, "I want to be top dog, not a donator."

"A what?" I say.

He looks my way as if I'm stupid. "A donator. A loser who pays his entry fee to perform in a rodeo but never wins any of the prize money that's shared by contestants who finish at the top. So a donator don't win shit, he just donates his entry fee to the winners." Then Poke leans back with his hands behind his head and that dreamy look again.

We lie around swatting bugs and sweating, and suddenly Poke says, "But I'd agree to ride slack before becoming a star. Yeah, I can see me and Spooky doing that when we start out."

"Okay," I say. "I give up. What the hell is 'slack?'"

Poke gets this superior grin announcing he's about to tell me something I don't know, ignorant bastard that I am. He likes doing that. He rises partway off the ground and leans on one elbow, a blade of grass between his front teeth. "When you're 'slack' you're one of the contestants who competes outside the regular rodeo performances, usually early in the morning when only the professionals is wandering around the paddocks or sitting the railings bullshitting and watching the slackers. Slack don't pay, but it's a chance to get established on the circuit and start making a name for yourself and your horse."

I would never swell Poke's head by telling this, but horses are kind of interesting to me in an abstract way. I've seen them in Central Park pulling buggies with tourists riding on the seats. Those were times when my friends and I went over to Manhattan on the subway. We'd go to just hang around watching the other pedestrians, stopping along the street when we got hungry to enjoy a hot slice with pepperoni. But *ride* a horse? I've never even touched one. For me, climbing on top of a horse would be as unlikely as volunteering to play violin at Carnegie Hall, and I've never touched a violin either. There's some things in life you don't need to do.

I liked when Poke talked about pasture grasses, a subject more in line with my interests than horses. Apparently Texas has many native grasses, and ranchers plant several more that aren't native but superior in some respects. His pa doesn't plant these foreign varieties because of the extra work and expense, although doing so would allow him to run more cattle on his limited acreage. But he figures what he has is sufficient. I learned that some grasses are superior in hot weather, others in winter.

Poke's pa rotates pastures so some sections are allowed to mature into hay they cut, bale, and store in the hayloft of the barn to use as winter forage. They rely largely on alfalfa, which isn't a grass but a perennial legume, and would like to plant rye grass, except it's an annual. Add to this the expense of the seed and time spent harrowing. Another good choice is Bermuda grass, but it has to be transplanted and can't be sown. That makes it labor-intensive. They mow their pastures before seedhead formation when new leaves stop forming. Then the plant builds up fiber and becomes less digestible, and protein percentage starts to decline. I didn't know about any of this.

Poke, his pa, and Jorge fertilize the pastures on occasion. The soil at Los Ebanos is sandy, making potassium deficiency a big problem. With grasses the more nitrogen the better because nitrogen stimulates vegetative growth. According to Poke spreading a couple of hundred pounds of nitrogen per acre could result in nearly seven tons of hay. To save money on fertilizer they spread manure over pastures scheduled to be fallow. They get the manure from shoveling out the barn. Not having attended an agriculture college, almost everything Poke tells me is new information. Poke is surely single-minded and not qualified to talk about much, but on the subject of ranching he knows a helluva lot.

Hillbilly

Poke says to me, "You got a woman back home in Hicksville?" He says it while whirling around a toothpick in his mouth. Poke is always chewing on a toothpick. He's always humping a box of toothpicks. Don't ask me why, he just does. I don't ever think of him without a toothpick or at least a blade of grass in his mouth.

"Yeah I got me one," I say.

"She got a name?"

I take my time untying and pulling my boots off and then peeling off my socks, which are wet and stink bad. My feet, like everyone's feet out here, are soft and wrinkled. They've turned a unnatural white. Even Bunny's feet are a lighter color than the rest of him. It's unnatural. The LT makes us take off our foot clothes every few days and then comes around and checks our feet for jungle rot. If it's let go too long your feet turn black and gangrenous and have to be amputated; wait even longer and the infection travels up through your whole body and you die. Nobody on the fireteam has black feet, not yet at least. "Twyla Ray," I say.

"What kind of a name is that?" Poke says.

"The kind they give you when you're borned, I guess." I keep looking at my feet and shrug like there's nothing I can do about it. "That's her name," I say.

"It's a weird name," Poke says.

I don't answer because when you think about it every name is weird in its way. Maybe she's the first to be named Twyla Ray, but there always has to be a first, don't there? If it warn't there couldn't be a second or a third. I don't see why it matters besides, a name being just a label we use to identify one another, like these labels sewed onto our shirts and such. I wish I could go home.

Thoughts, if that is what they were, seemed like pieces of interrupted memories climbing over each other in a rush to be seen and heard. That's how they seemed. Mama's coffee can of bacon grease kept for frying on the window sill beside the stove where she stood and looked out at the train tracks, an English ivy growing in a glass of water beside it trailing down. Every so often she poured out the old water, refilled the glass, and set it back. I ast her once why she never put that plant in a pot of dirt. She said because she liked seeing its roots—them anchors God give to it that he hides underground—and not just its top.

The LT has just told us to assemble. Still barefoot we hobble to a small clearing. He's going to give us a quick talk about alertness, the same one he gives us every few days when he decides we're getting tired and careless from too long in the bush. It's about IEDs and trip wires which, as he reminds us, cause more casualties than enemy fire. Lots of times IEDs are made using our own ordnance, in this case M61 fragmentation hand grenades, which all of us carry. We're trained to arm a grenade if the enemy's position is within throwing distance, rear back, and throw it. The M61 weighs exactly a pound, and a typical grunt supposedly can chuck one about forty meters. They tell us that, but I doubt it. The grenade's steel housing disintegrates into its own shrapnel on impact,. Killing radius is about fifteen meters, although fragments can disperse up to two hundred-thirty meters. Accuracy ain't that important. As the LT says, you don't have to hit the catcher's mitt dead center, just get it to the general area of the strike zone.

In common language, what's killed is anything, man or animal, within fifty feet of the explosion. Some guys die on the spot, others bleed out waiting to be evac'd. Maybe you get your arms or legs blowed off. Whatever happens ain't pretty. As the LT never tires of telling us, we're so far out in the boonies that any serious wound and a Marine is dead meat by the time a chopper can get here, especially when as short as we are. We don't have enough men to make a squad, much less take along a corpsman. We're still waiting to get one. The Marines is always shorthanded. A Few Good Men seems about right. Too few if you ast me. So count on dying if you don't stay alert. Plan on going home in a glad bag, and that's no shit.

We learn this stuff in basic, of course, or later on in field training, but the LT thinks repetition is important to keep us on high alert. I might be the only one back home in Scalded Creek, West Virginia, who has ever used the word "meter," unless you're talking about a water meter. To make the term clear the LT says to think of a meter as the same as a yard, and that throwing forty meters is about like standing just inside the end zone on a football field and having it bounce on the forty yard line. Now, that's a helluva long distance, but once he explained it the whole thing made sense. I wish someone had told us earlier how far forty meters was.

Charlie uses our own stuff to kill us. Not only our ordnance but our actual junk. Wherever we go we leave junk behind, and lots of it is useful to the enemy. Baling wire from C-rat cases can be used to make trip wires to kill and wound our own guys somewhere down a trail. Empty C-rat cans become the housings of IEDs, some of the easiest and most effective booby traps the VC can make. And the actual device is often one or our own M61s that's been stole, recovered after a skirmish, or captured. All you do is slip out the cotter pin and compress the safety lever as if you're about to throw it, but instead you shove it into a tin can tight enough to keep the lever compressed. Then you attach one end of a thin wire to the grenade, snug the tin can underneath some trailside vegetation, and tie the other end of the wire to a tree or shrub across the trail opposite.

The trick is to stretch it across the path low to the ground and camouflage its entire length with a layer of leaf litter and twigs. Then along comes a grunt walking point who trips over the ankle-high wire, which pulls the grenade out of the can and arms it, and after a five-second delay, BOOM! A dead or wounded point man, maybe more than one if his comrades is bunched up close behind.

We sometimes retaliate with our own booby traps using two grenades across a trail from one another. For the trip and lever tie-down "wire" we use dental floss pulled across a stick of cammie grease paint, which makes it resemble a thin green vine. Sometimes we cut short lengths of bamboo, pound them into the ground as anchors, and covered them with debris. If we've brought any white-phosphorous grenades we use them instead of the M61s, or link one of each in a combo. When white phosphorus hits the skin it don't quit until it's burned a hole clear through. Nasty stuff, but if we don't use it on the gooks they'll just use it on us.

The LT's little talk ends by reminding us that war is important because the higher-highers tell us so. They need something to do while sitting in their air-conditioned offices in Saigon. The LT tells us to remember that writing great books and inventing life-saving drugs is difficult undertakings, but killing other human beings is a breeze, no harder than climbing a tree over there and knocking down the fruit. He gestures at the rainforest where several monkeys is shaking the branches and shrieking. "It's just a different way of fucking the dog," he says. Then, like he always does, he reminds us: "There is no God, so we've assembled here to praise war, mindless lust, and the continuance of stupidity."

"Amen," we answer in unison.

Injun

That first day when I came up behind them the guys looked at me real strange, like I was something out of a western movie. Later, after I'd got to know them, one guy named Poke actually said that. He said, "Jesus Christ, man, I thought you was a actual Indian. I was expecting to see the Lone Ranger pop out of the woods behind you. It was weird, really weird." I told him I am an actual Indian, but it didn't change the look he gave me.

I guess I did appear strange to a fireteam of grunts: out of uniform, barefoot, not carrying a weapon. First thing the LT did was tug me close to him by my neck chain, peel the tape off my dog tags, and read them to confirm I'm who I claimed I am. Then he says to this Poke dude, the RO humping the radio, "Get base Force Recon Company on the horn. I want to speak with the Actual." This is military for the top duty dog. The Poke dude does as he's told. The LT then gets on the horn and says, like, "This is First Squad Actual." He gives the rest of the standard boiler plate bullshit to identify himself, then says, "I think we got one of yours, except he looks like. . .well, I don't know what he looks like."

The Actual at the other end then says, "Don't tell me. Injun, right?"

"Uh, Roger that," says the LT. "What should I do with him?"

"Keep him for the time being. I never met the dude but hear tales he'll do right by you. My predecessor hated his guts and thought he ought to be court martialed for desertion and insubordination, but he rotated out months ago. Anyhow Injun's former team members admit they deserted him, not vice versa, because both Injun and the previous Actual wanted it that way. I say let him do his thing. I checked. You're short some men, so you could probably use him. I mean, what the hell's a lieutenant doing running a fireteam, for chrissakes? Understand that one day he'll disappear on you. He'll just be gone. Don't go looking because you'll never find him. Fucker's like the wind. We've never found him either, and we're fucking Recon, but he'll fucking eventually find one of our patrols if wants to. Bottom line? He isn't AWOL, he's just a, uh, independent contractor of sorts." The base Actual laughed, making the radio crackle.

"He doesn't appreciate clothes, even boots, as I'm sure you've already seen. Maybe he knows more than the rest of us. He probably doesn't have immersion foot, or that's my guess. I'll wager he doesn't have jungle rot on him anywhere. We should ship him back to Walter Reed to use as a specimen, maybe make some clones. Think of it: fireteams of bush Marines without jungle rot. Oh, and let him walk point whenever he wants, which according to his file is always, and take him along when you patrol the perimeter at night. Do that and maybe everybody stays alive and comes back with his balls intact. Over and out."

So here I am with a batch of common grunts from Alpha Company who don't know jack-shit about Recon and what we do. In a way they're retards. No special training, no clue about how to survive in the bush without regular air-drops of C-rats and ammo. Babies shuffling along blind to everything. Babies still needing the tit. They stroll down enemy trails too lazy to bushwhack new ones, something Recons seldom do. That's inviting a booby trap. Recons reconnoiter enemy trails, we don't use them as sidewalks. You didn't make the trail? Then stay the hell off it. No wonder so many grunts get sent home in glad bags.

They also never learn to smell, see, hear, touch the land and feel its rhythms. Use your senses to capacity and it's so easy to locate the human intruders, to isolate the individual perpetrators and kill them one by one. Silently. Leaving their remains to dissolve into compost, their volatile components to dissipate on the wind.

If I've learned one thing since being here it's that in worshipping the land the Vietnamese convinced themselves they know and understand it, but they're wrong. Thousands of years of occupying a place mean nothing. It's the land that knows them instead. It senses them breathing, coughing, talking, and in the end consumes and absorbs each one. Farmers bury their dead in the rice paddies to fertilize the soil for the next generation, like it's based on some Confucian wisdom. Does the land care? It never asked to be a rice field. Want the land to be contented? Then disappear. My own contribution is minor: I merely aid the land in the timeless task of reclaiming itself from humanity.

Bunny

A nickname, even a dumb one, doesn't take getting used to if you've had it all your life. I've had mine since I was a baby, practically since I was born. My older sister Evelyn gave it to me. When she and Mom took me outdoors in cold weather they put a funny little wool cap on my head. The cap, which they got at a thrift shop, was cheap and poorly made and had a couple of points on top that stuck up in the air. Evelyn was seven or eight, and according to Mom everything made her giggle, especially me. She thought the points on that cap looked like rabbit ears and so she started calling me Bunny. The name stuck. In high school I stood six-feet-five inches and weighed two-twenty, and I was still Bunny to everyone. It's likely only a few people in the neighborhood even know my real name, including most of my friends.

We live in the Morrisania neighborhood, South Bronx. It's a mean place. Crime is rampant; nearly all residents are black. I suppose the cops at the 42nd Precinct do their best to keep order, but their best isn't nearly good enough. It seems every day people get shot and killed, either targeted in the endless gang wars or because they're just in the wrong place, what the military over here in 'Nam calls "collateral fatalities." The term describes both situations perfectly. Either way a "civilian" is killed or injured, someone who never asked for a war and wishes only to be left alone in safety.

By the time I reached Evelyn's age she was already lost to the streets, so I never really knew her, not the Evelyn who giggled at everything, not the sister who named me Bunny. By then she had dropped out of school and was a heroin addict. At first she came home when she needed money or just a quiet place to cry. There was no humor in her life, nothing worth giggling about. Mom was working two jobs mopping floors. Evelyn would watch our building and come around after Mom left for work and to steal stuff to sell for drugs. She still carried a key to the apartment. Mom eventually had to get the lock changed. After that we seldom saw Evelyn except occasionally on the street panhandling. Eventually she disappeared. We never knew what became of her, although when I was older I'd sometimes look for her in the alleys and side streets. I'd check out every young woman who was down and out, hoping she would be Evelyn and I could save her. And I rehearsed what I'd say when that moment came. I'd say, "We love you, Ev. Mom and I love and miss you. Please come home and let's be a family again." But of course I never got the chance. When I was small I thought the harder I rehearsed this little speech—the more sincere I sounded—the more likely the odds I'd find Evelyn. You keep reasoning like this until adulthood teaches that hope and logic occupy separate universes.

We have two grainy photos of Ev. One is her baby picture on Mom's bureau. The other is on my desk at home. That one shows the two of us standing together on the sidewalk out front squinting into the sun. We're holding hands and smiling. I must have been about 2. She's wearing a pale summer dress. Like the baby picture, it's in black and white. Mom tells me Ev's dress was pink. To see what the other colors might have been I had only to step outdoors. She's always in my mind, that sister, always a little girl in a pink dress, never the aged and hollow-eyed ghost she became.

Dad departed for the streets before I was born. We have no pictures of him, and Mom has never told me anything about him. She might have loved him once, but in the end he was nothing but a sperm donor. I've never tried to find my father. What would be the point? Maybe I've passed him staring out the entrance to a trash-blown alley or looked into his rheumy eyes when he asked me for a dime on a street corner. Maybe he was that lump of old clothes cradling a bottle of rot-gut wine on the subway grate just down the street. If so I passed him on the way to school and back for maybe a year until one day he wasn't there. Maybe he became a John Doe in one of the city morgues.

I know this: Mom was determined to save me regardless of personal cost. Her only goal was to get me educated and out of the projects. Out of public housing and its roaches and rats, away from the crime and drugs. I was equally determined to leave, in large part because in prospering I could save her too, take her along into another, safer, life. Football opened the door.

I'd wanted to attend Fordham right there in the Bronx. It was close to the botanical garden, close enough to home that I could keep one eye on Mom and the other still scanning the streets for my sister. My high school grades were good, and I'd never been in trouble, but Fordham didn't show any interest. The one offer I got was from a small Protestant college in Tennessee. I'd never heard of the place. One day during my senior year the football coach stopped me in the hall and said a coach from this school wanted to interview me, and so I met him after my last class. We went to the gym and sat together in the bleachers.

He was an overweight white guy with grizzled hair. "Everett," he said, "I've checked you out. I'm prepared to offer you a free ride to Tennessee Christian State, but I got to tell you up front that you'll be one of the only colored kids there. The college ain't officially segregated, but in ath–a–letics we ain't encouraged to recruit minorities. Just telling you up front. And by the way, call me Coach."

You could tell the guy had once been regular–size by his feet, which were small and encased in shiny

Italian shoes with pointed ends. He pulled out a pack of butts and lit one, inhaling deeply. I could smell a hint of liquor on him and he needed a shave, but otherwise he seemed normal enough. It was my first experience alone with a white man. I didn't say anything for a minute or so, then I said, "Call me Bunny."

He jerked his head around and looked directly at me. "*Bunny*? A guy your size?" Then he laughed and said, "Oh, I get it, like in Jungle Bunny, right?"

That sort of hit me between the eyes. I'd frankly never considered the connection. In my neighborhood lots of guys address each other as "nigger," as in, hey nigger, wassup? I never paid much attention, but with all the civil rights stuff happening in the Deep South even the youngest of us knew "nigger" to be among the most incendiary racist epithets. It occurred to me for the first time, sitting there in the gym watching some other black kids dribble around a basketball, that a black person calling another of his race a nigger might be okay, but it wasn't when used by someone who's white.

I took a breath and said, "No sir, nothing like that. My sister named me Bunny when I was a baby because she thought it was cute, and it stuck."

"Well, don't take what I said personal," Coach said. "I ain't prejudiced." He took a drag on his cigarette and glanced away, relieved but still uncomfortable.

"It's okay," I said.

Coach said, "Look, I don't care what color a guy is—white, black, red, or whatever, so long as he can play football. My job is coaching football and winning games. I won't blow smoke up your ass. Tennessee has some racial prejudice, but so do lots of other places. Me? I ain't a Southerner. I'm from Pennsylvania, but you take coaching jobs where you find them." Then he added sagely, "And as for the race thing, it ain't likely to get better until it does."

I didn't say anything because I was thinking, this would be the most important decision of my life until now. My silence must have made him uncomfortable.

"And don't worry about the studies," he said. "We got a P.E. program the guys all enroll in, and the Phys Ed Department is entirely in our camp. They understand we have to keep guys eligible. With your grades the studies will come easy." He dropped the butt and ground it out.

"I'm thinking of majoring in biology," I said. "I want to be a botanist."

He looked at me strangely. "A botanist?"

"Yes, the study of plants."

"You mean trees and flowers and stuff?"

"Them too. Did you bring a catalog listing the curriculum for biology?"

"Uh, sure I did, but nobody's ever asked to see it before." He rummaged around in the tattered briefcase at his feet and finally found it. There it was, the biology curriculum listed by semester for all four years, including the chemistry, math, physics, and humanities requirements necessary to gain a bachelor of science degree.

I handed him back the catalog. "You pay all expenses? Lab fees too?"

"Everything. Room in the dorm, meal tickets to the cafeteria, even bus fare home when a semester ends and back to school when the next one starts. Books too. Let me see that curriculum."

He held the booklet at arm's length and looked at the two pages, lower lip jutting out as if appraising their content. "Shit, you really want to be studying when you could be taking P.E. classes and hanging out with the guys on the team?"

"Yes, I do."

"He got up heavily as if his knees hurt. "Well, if you can play offensive tackle and stay eligible, it's no skin off my ass, long as studying and classwork don't interfere with football. We expect a return on these scholarships." He handed me a business card. "Here's my phone number. Go home, talk it over with your family, and give me a call if you decide to commit. I'll keep the scholarship open two weeks, no more. I got a team to put together."

I went home and talked it over with Mom. Coach was still recruiting and wouldn't be back in his office for the rest of the week, but the next day I called and told his secretary I'd accepted.

The LT

When the black angel of death sweeps overhead and cries out for more light, how will *you* respond? He wishes to ask his men this question. He wants to tell them not to worry but instead embrace the anxiety, that the boot impressions pressed into the muddy bottoms of their fighting holes were from the weight of their dreams. He wants them to feel what he felt in his first firefight, an unexplainable thrill of touching the untouchable, seeing what mortals are told is impossible to see. The unexplainable, by definition, can't be explained. Obvious, but like all tautologies, it's also truthful. He's afraid of frightening them and of losing their trust when they decide he's crazy.

He understands something the military knows only at a rudimentary level. Both realize that in war you persevere. In war you *react*. There's indeed a difference between the quick and soon-to-be-dead. But only he and a few colleagues could describe the mechanism: fast reactions over many repetitions fine-tune the brain's subgenual anterior cingulate cortex (sgACC), and experienced fighters can make potentially life-saving decisions even six or seven seconds before consciously aware of danger. He knows this from having measured it personally in laboratory subjects.

The war had interrupted the research before it could be replicated, so it was never published. It would remain undiscovered until his team members could reassemble. Had they advised the military their findings would have been received with predictable apathy. Nothing else was required to make it vaporize. This form of knowledge they had uncovered is semantic, having been memorized. With intense training and frequent repetition the brain self-organizes until reaction precedes decision.

We believe ourselves capable of doing more than one thing at a time, but that's illusion. The conscious brain can actually only process one item, which means that processing several must be done sequentially. When presented with several targets a trained rifleman selects them singly in rapid sequence. Length of the refractory period between targets is to a large extent a matter of training and reinforcement of that training, which includes a learned ability to continue focusing without distraction.

He knows that the key to staying alive in a fast-twitch situation like a firefight is response time. Dimly understanding this the military puts you through "immediate-action drills" during which you repetitively focus on perceive-interpret-react. The stimulus in combat is a blast of dopamine. Intense military training can set the brain on alert, but if stimulus-releasing events never attain culmination the dopamine response attenuates.

So what does intense training mimicking combat achieve? Retention of perseverance, forcing the trainees to press on in anticipation of an actual event, at which time the sgACC might perhaps save the life of its owner or a comrade. This is why he ragged on his men continuously to *stay alert*. Would you rather remain among the quick or join the dead?

He's prepared to ask them the all-important question, but knows he won't: how will you feel in combat? Here's how; listen up. Too small, too soft, too slow. You'll think if only you were bigger and armor-plated and faster you could overcome the enemy's artillery and once behind his lines, outrun him. He longs to advise them that if they're destined to die, do it quickly. Don't linger, don't wait to be overtaken by gangrene and other agonies. Don't lose your life's-blood to the earth drop by drop. Finally, put to rest forever this exilic longing for home, some specific location on a map signifying comfort. Such places no longer exist and perhaps never did. We can never go home, even in spirit. You've stepped into another universe from which you can't go back. You motherfuckers don't exist. This place, this time, this war, all is illusion. Get used to it. Get used to being no one. You have a sweaty ass and jungle rot? It isn't real, just nerve endings squeaking.

He aches to tell them that no military force is ever more powerful than its antagonist. The victor is whichever first consumes the other's imagination. A death in battle, he'll say, subtracts a life but circumvents the later sickness and suffering. He yearns to tell them about death. He's seen it up close, felt its rough scales brush against his skin, looked into its empty yellow eye. My gracious, what a sight, beautiful in its horror, and an odor you wouldn't believe. It had been his hope by some reptilian logic to experience that defining truth only war can reveal and afterward survive more or less intact. And he had.

He knows all this, but he also knows his prospective audience is young. The thing about life is the requirement of movement over time. Not simply eye blinks, tongue flaps, and fornication, but also pulsation, cell division, meiosis, tissue differentiation, so the balls don't end up where a heart is supposed to grow. Try telling this to a nineteen-year-old Marine exhausted and sleep-deprived, hungry, horny, and homesick. Better to explain how everything is possible, little is probable, and randomness is usually an excuse to hide fuckups. Uniformity in nature is rare. Wrap up everything you just thought and put it in comforting terms they understand: what matters is whether you're getting laid. Leave the rest to me.

In keeping quiet is he being fair? Nothing is unconditional. In not posing his question is the LT a man of honor by sparing their fears, or does it make him a dishonorable man by not being open? That could depend in part on how honor is defined. Honor is an abstraction, an idea, a human invention and matter of culture. Is the LT a man of substance? That depends upon whether substance refers to skin and bone, ligament and muscle; whether it manifests as physical *density*. If so, then yes, he's a man of substance, but substance is susceptible ultimately to the degradation of rot and decay, to concealing itself in the anonymity of dissolution and ultimately merging with what blows past on the wind. The LT is trapped in infinite regress, never to arrive at what he hoped was a moral destination, a place recognized by agency.

In a firefight the mind and body can decouple, the mind undergoing an out-of-body experience. At such moments the ego hovers nearby like a detached soul, watching dispassionately. It observes the body in slow motion as it runs, stumbles, waves an arm, fires a weapon; it sees the mouth opening to emit a scream, although what emerges is oddly mute. He wondered afterward when all had returned to normal if there had even been a propagated pressure wave. If so, he thought, then my disembodied ego is either deaf or nonexistent, assuming only the tangible or the living can feel the effect and therefore hear.

Time impedes the prospect of impending death, some of it transferred to space where it slows for the person perceiving it. Thus the effects of motion on time become fused into the furious four-dimensional void of spacetime. Past, present, and future can't be distinguished. You become aware that every moment already exists, and existence itself is illusion. According to physics, time's arrow can be reversed, causing events to run backward by reversing velocity. Events move from order to disorder; the processes with time. Prediction does not contradict observation.

Now switch to the second person and see how descriptive resolution sharpens. Other human forms also occupy that scene, many or perhaps just a few. Impossible to tell because the focus is entirely on the simulation of your physical being, an instantiated moiety of your mythical "self." The other moiety, as we know from out-of-body experiences, has been relegated to observer status. The rest of the scene is dark, the participants only shadows.

While in this half-and-half state the senses heighten to levels never previously experienced. Colors are brighter, explosions strangely muffled and far away as if the land preserves an echoic memory. In the body being watched, haptic sensations surge through every capillary and muscle fiber causing them to bulge and retract in unison, to resonate like guitar strings. Time retreats, stretches, and holds. This is you feeling the suspended tension of immortality; for the first time you experience *now*—a lifetime compressed into an instant.

Nothing until this moment has been important. Beside it even the prospect of death is trivial. What happened? For a nanosecond your consciousness expanded beyond the ego's impervious walls. That first-person "I" of your mythical self just captured what mystics spend a lifetime chasing, a glimpse of the opulent, transcendent world beyond the barrier of ordinary human sensations. Call it Nirvana or anything you like. Its defining quality is merely that it renounces definition.

Then instantaneously, in the time it took to arrive, it's gone. Mind and body suddenly conflate; the fragile wave-function of *now* collapses into the mundane and familiar. You can hear the shouts and screams, the rifle fire and whistle of incoming artillery, the load hurtling toward you, its whine increasing like God's lament at sending his angel of death. Sennacherib's angel had come on wings as silent as an owl's, barely a disruption of the universe, a puff of his breath sufficient to annihilate an army. This angel arrived with an ear-splitting voice shrieking its presence.

The revelation you experienced is undeniable, what veterans mean but can't articulate when they say you had to be there to understand, how war is so deeply visceral, so alive and sensual that no description could ever be adequate. It isn't something invented in the merging of silences. For the rest of their lives they'll yearn to again feel *now* rushing past, while denying its loss to the great churning maelstrom of future and past. In place of acceptance they'll reminisce, get drunk, laugh and cry over old photos, do anything to recapture that infinitesimal moment when the gates to infinity swung open revealing the playground of the gods. But *now* has become a frayed memory stuck out of time, and chasing after it no less futile than netting stardust. Their singular *now* has been subsumed in uncountable *nows* born simultaneously at the edges of a universe expanding at lightspeed where new space and new time are created endlessly.

Poke

Me and Bunny was having one of our talks, the kind where he talks to me then me to him, back and forth. I was telling him about Spooky, who's about fourteen hands high, a proper size for a stock horse, but small by some standards. A horse's size depends on how you intend to use him, among other things, and the smaller, nimbler ones is often superior for cutting and roping. Anyhow I was saying how I thought Spooky would be about the right size of a horse for me, a smaller guy in terms of rodeo. I'm built lean and wiry like Buzz Peth, who stands five-foot-seven and weighs maybe one-forty-five, one-fifty. I've never knowed Buzz personal, never met the gentleman, but I feel almost like me and him, we're kindred spirits and I can call him by his first name.

So we're laying back on a patch of wet ground taking a break, me and Bunny, and I'm puffing away on a cigarette. Bunny used to be a football player and don't smoke. He tells me it takes your wind away from you, but what the hell do I care at this point? When he tells me smoking is bad for my health I ast him if he thinks Vietnam is good for it. Every grunt humps mosquito repellent with instructions on the cans not to inhale it. Us inhale it or the mosquitoes, we joke. Fuck it, we could be dead any second.

But I'm getting off the subject. As I said, me and Bunny and the rest of the fireteam is laying on this patch of ground, which in monsoon season is always wet, it don't make a fucking bit of difference where it is, and me and him, we're shooting the shit when all of a sudden Bunny says, "Think I could be a cowboy?" I'm sort of speechless because to tell the truth I'd never thought about any of the other guys working professional in rodeo.

Then I laugh and start to cough at the same time, as some people do when they're embarrassed and try to cover up a laugh with a cough to show they ain't really laughing at you, just coughing. But that wasn't me at the time. I really had been laughing and then really started to cough. When I finally quit doing both I said, "No, it ain't very likely."

I'd said what I meant, but Bunny took it wrong, regardless. He got testy and said "Because there's only white cowboys, huh?"

And I said, "No, fool, that ain't what I meant. Rufus Green Senior is one of the most famous rodeo cowboys of all time, and he's black. I meant you could never be one 'cause you're so goddamn big. You'd never find a horse with enough size and agility to compete, you dumb shit." Bunny didn't say nothing, but I could tell he felt a little better.

As I said, Bunny graduated college. He's a smart dude. I ain't disputing that, but there's some shit he don't get, like the technology of calf roping. Just the other day after we'd quit the hump and found a harbor site I set down with a stick in my hand and drawed him a picture in the dirt. It was a calf-roping arena at your average rodeo as seen if you was setting on a cloud above it or hanging out a chopper hovering overhead. I showed him how the calves line up in a narrow runway nose to tail. The first one is let into the "chute," which is like a box with doors that can be raised in front and back. The door behind blocks off the other calves waiting their turn. The one in front opens into the arena. The chute is small, too narrow for the calf to turn around. Rodeo workers tie a light rope about thirty feet long around the animal's neck. The other end is attached to a trip-lever.

The roper waits on his horse behind a rope barrier. When ready he calls for the calf. The chute-man raises the door, and the calf runs into the arena giving it a head start on the roper. Soon as it hits the end of the rope the lever trips, dropping the rope barrier behind where the rider and horse wait and simultaneously the rope around the calf's neck falls off. At this instant the clock starts ticking, and the chase is on. The horse accelerates from standing to a gallop.

I pause a second and then add that if the horse breaks too soon the rider receives a ten-second penalty, which usually puts him out of the money. They call this a "cowboy speeding ticket." I laugh, but

Bunny looks at me like he don't get the joke. Maybe he's tired from the day's hump or he's just in a sour mood. Maybe it's because he's a city boy and ain't got a sense of humor.

Anyways while astride his horse the rider throws his lariat over the calf's head. The "lariat" of course is his calf-rope. When there's a slip-knot in the business end it's called a "lasso." So in other words a lasso is also a lariat, but not always the other way around. When the calf's done been lassoed the rider signals his horse to stop, which a good roping horse does on a dime. Not just stop, but digs its rear hooves into the dirt floor of the arena. It's why good roping horses need to have strong hindquarters. The horse's job is to hold the rope taut after the rider cinches the part remaining in his hand around the saddle horn in a clove hitch, jumps to the ground, throws the calf on its side, and ties up three of its legs in a "hooey" using his "piggin' string." What we call a "hooey" is just a half-hitch. The "piggin' string" is a soft rope about six feet long. The instant the calf is what they call "immobilized" the rider raises both hands in the air, a signal to the timer to stop the clock. Professionals like Dan Taylor and Shoat Webster can complete the whole sequence, chute release to tied piggin' string, in seven seconds or a little less.

When I say how quick they done it Bunny don't say a goddamn thing, like he ain't impressed, which hurts my feelings a little. Guess we both stomped each other's feelings on the same day. But now that I think about it, the way Bunny don't appreciate how fast a professional calf roper can be and then wouldn't laugh at my joke sort of pissed me off, actually.

Injun

I fell in several meters behind their tail-end Charlie before anyone knew it and could have stayed with them all day undetected. I don't know how long I've been on my own, but months. I've seen the seasons change and the cycle start again, and no doubt I'm well past the date when I could have rotated out and back to the World. How did I come to be alone and out of uniform? I ain't AWOL, which I want to make clear.

It happened like this. I'm on patrol with my Recon fireteam one day, and I tell the staff sergeant I'm sick of the scene. He says he's equally sick of me. We're taking a break after humping all morning. We've just staged our gear and are unpacking some lunch. The guys are laying around enjoying a break from the rain.

"Okay," says this lifer of a Mother Green motherfucker. "Hang tight." He tells the RO to get base company Actual on the horn, that he wants to call in a situation report.

The Actual hates my guts because I don't suck

up to authority. The Actual listens then says to the staff sergeant, "Bring him in and I'll see he gets a dishonorable discharge."

The asshole turns to me. "Hear that?" he says.

"Tell the Actual I don't want a fucking discharge of any kind. I want to be left alone to do my duty. Didn't I get sent here to kill VC? All we do in Recon is sneak around counting them and listening to them jabber."

The Actual hears this and gets truly pissed. He orders the staff sergeant to let me go. He says it just like that: "Let the fucker go. If he can navigate back to base without a map, then good for him. If he can't, fuck him. Take his rifle and gear and redistribute them. Mark him down as MIA if the rest of the squad agrees. If there's a single dissent you bring him back and his ass is mine, hear me? Over and out." The others agree in a heartbeat. It appears I'm not popular with even my peers, as if I give a good goddamn. I'm thinking, *me* get lost in the woods? What a fucking joke. I ain't the one who needs a map and compass.

"So," the staff sergeant says, "you've now relinquished your weapon and other gear. You're still a Marine, and I hate leaving you here because you're sure to get smoked by the VC, so I'm giving you a choice of at least a garrote or brass knuckles. You'll need to defend yourself. Keep the dog tags so we can eventually identify your remains. Take the K-knife, shirt, trousers, and boots, and your cigarette lighter. That's it. Anything loose in your pockets, take that too."

I tell him, "Give me a garrote and what you

already listed, but keep the shirt, boots, and all that other shit. I travel light." He didn't argue. The guys stood around while I stripped down and cut off the trouser legs. After finishing their smokes they saddled up and left without eating lunch or even saying goodbye. They were probably thinking, good job Marine, kill some VC on your own. It's a suicide mission you wanted, now choke on it. We'll see the remains of your sorry ass next time through, but we won't go looking for them. They meant, die you fucker. Skulk off like a stray dog and just die. We'll come across your tags eventually. Meanwhile we're tired of your shit.

We'd been moving through a valley looking for an artillery placement thought to be near a ville a few more klicks east. This setup was supposedly righteousness constrained in an artillery tube, a metallic something alien to the forest still unfolding and floral and dripping, and they had sent us to find it. They abandoned me near a field of elephant grass. I had my cigarette lighter and my stash. I sat on the ground and got stoned, feeling relaxed for the first time in memory.

The more I stared at that elephant grass the more it started resembling sawgrass. I got to wondering if I was back home in the Everglades and might come across Ma and Pa out hunting gators, but knew deep down that couldn't be true. Join up, they'd told me. Go see the great wide world. But how wide can the world be when one of your brightest memories so far is of a dog lapping puke on a village path? How's that for a tenderized moment poised and set to turn back and examine its own rectum? Oh Lordy, I thought, why does civilization always stink of piss? Truth is, someone would soon be hunting me. I already sensed his distant footfalls; I could almost smell the cabbage and fish sauce on his breath.

I had to prepare myself. I started by moving up out of the valley and foraging in the jungle of the highlands. I also ate what I took from VC I killed and what I could steal by sneaking into villes. When my diet changed the leeches dropped away and left me alone, same as happens to Seminoles in the Glades when they eat off the land. The bottoms of my feet got nice and calloused, and the jungle rot eventually healed itself. What I appreciated most is the silence of being by myself if only to hide inside the holes of my rags. I don't get lonely, don't need Jimi Hendricks blasting in my head getting me all jittery and some dumbass jarhead NCO shouting orders.

I got into the habit of laying up in trailside trees waiting for VC patrols to pass underneath. The VC never look up, only ahead, behind, and sideways. They think they're quiet, how they disappear into the forest like a rat into the belly of a snake, but I'm quieter. I wait till they go by then drop down and grab the tail-end Charlie and garrote him. I make less noise than a caterpillar crawling through wet leaf litter. They're little fuckers, weak in the arms. Killing them is easy. Then I take his rice and fish sauce and cabbage. I could take his rifle and ammo too, except

I don't want or need them.

After I made myself visible to this fireteam I tell the LT and his grunts that I don't want their C-rats and canteen water. Keep them, I say. C-rats will kill you quicker than the VC. What you eat is why y'all got leeches and jungle rot. That and wearing clothes. I say, y'all got to live with the land, not fight it, but of course they think I'm full of shit.

Hillbilly

Want to hear about life on the hump? As they tell us from the beginning, going on patrol means being on the move. Everything comes down to what each man carries. There's three categories of gear: personal items, weapons, and food. Before the first couple of patrols the sergeants teach us how to organize gear and pack it proper, then afterwards we do it ourself and they check our work. These guys are old hands and know exactly what a grunt needs to hump while on patrol, so you better listen close. One older sergeant, a lifer, told me that good habits follow you around like a faithful dog. When he returns home from deployment he can't rummage in his toolbox looking for a Phillips head screwdriver without thinking about reaching for a safety pin or tin of aspirin in his rucksack.

After we're finished packing and fully geared up the sergeant makes us jump up and down one at a time. He listens for anything loose that clanks, squeaks, or rattles, any sound that could give away our position. If he hears something he makes us unpack, find the source, and secure it. Dog tags must be wrapped in non-reflective tape so they're noiseless.

It's amazing how much shit the experienced bush Marine can stuff into his rucksack or hang off his ammo belts. You're reminded to pack stuff the same way every time and memorize exactly where each item goes because you might have to locate something in the dark and do it quick. You can't waste time and make noise rooting in your rucksack or grabbing for ammo. Every item is important, every little thing something that might save your life. At first there's a million things to consider and you get confused, but once everything's firm in the mind you forget the details and stow your shit automatically.

Like packing personal items. You need a spare set of cammies, a toothbrush, cigarettes and a lighter, and all that kind of shit, which I won't go into because it's boring. I add a few plugs of Days o' Work chewing tobacco. There ain't many smoke breaks on patrol, and none at all at night, but you can always chew tobacco. Here's an interesting fact: nobody wears skivvies in the bush. All that sweating just leads to a quicker case of ass and crotch rot. So skivvies are left behind at base camp and saved for R & R when you can wear them with civvies and feel dressed up. And never bring along a white t-shirt because white is easily spotted by a sniper against the green of the jungle. Keep your colors dark, preferably green or camouflage.

Wear two pairs of socks as cushion against the humping because weight can be your biggest enemy.

Not tiring out and losing focus is critical. Fully loaded you'll be toting a rucksack weighing at least sixty pounds. Then there's your change of clothes plus water, food, rifle, ammo, grenades, and so forth.

Sometimes you're assigned to carry an important item for benefit of the whole team. Poke humps the PRC-77 radio, which weighs fourteen pounds not counting batteries. Bunny humps a M79 grenade launcher called a "blooper" because of the sound it makes when fired. It's only about six pounds, but he also lugs the ammo for it. That's in addition to his M-16 and its ammo. I carry some claymore mines and the receiver used to set the perimeter at night. None of this shit you'd call light, and the combined weight has a way of pushing down on your feet. Like they say, if your feet wasn't flat when you joined up, they will be when you muster out. I advise carrying two extra pairs of socks if you got the space. There might actually be a chance to wash out a first pair. And don't forget taping your pants at the ankles to help keep out the leeches or they'll climb up your legs and devour your balls. And for that, of course, you need to carry a roll of tape.

Finally there's food and water to consider. Each guy humps his own. A bush Marine typically carries three or four canteens and enough C-rats for his esti-mated time in the field plus a little extra. For patrols of a week or more we might bring "long-rats" too, dehydrated meals you mix with canteen water and heat. A case of C-rats contains twelve meals. Some of this includes cans of "heavies" like spaghetti, meat and potatoes, and chicken. They add weight to your rucksack, but big guys like Bunny need the calories. Because you sweat like a pig you're always thirsty, and once the canteen water is used up you're looking to replace it with rainwater from a puddle or stream. So you don't get dysentery on top of the dysentery you already got you carry halazone tablets to drop in jungle water. Leaves a terrible taste, but what the hell.

I don't hump heavies, but I mentioned that Bunny does. He eats them first to lighten his rucksack as we go along. He brings lots of grape jelly, which he mixes with everything, even spaghetti and his meat and potatoes. Chocolate too, if he's brought any. Poke humps a bottle of hot sauce his sister buys south of the border and mails to him. I put a drop on my tongue once and it damn near burned a hole through it. Poke spreads this shit on everything. You get used to the heat, he says. He tells us that a Mexican don't know he's hungry until his asshole quits burning. It's a Texas joke, he says, in case we don't get it.

In Mother Green lingo the place you bivouac at night when on patrol is a "harbor site." If the vegetation is thick and the LT feels reasonably sure the enemy is nowhere in earshot we clear a "field of fire" around the harbor site with a machete before establishing a perimeter. It might extend only a few meters out, but even this amount of open space might be enough to expose Charlie creeping up.

A perimeter at a harbor site can be established

several ways depending on available equipment, the terrain, weather, and so forth. We use PSIDs (Personnel Seismic Intrusion Devices), called "pee-sids." The setup requires four battery-operated transmitters and a receiver and is designed to detect ground movements. It operates on coded signals sent to the receiver. Signals are inaudible; the only way to hear them is through the receiver.

Once inside the harbor site we send out two guys with the pee-sids to secure the four compass points of the perimeter. At each place they shove a pee-sid into the earth, which isn't too difficult because it's usually mud, set a claymore anti-personnel mine on top of it, and camouflaged the site with leaf litter. A claymore mine delivers seven hundred steel balls in a fan-shaped array at groin height of a standing man, so they are aimed outward away from the perimeter. When you finish the only visible projection is the pee-sid's antenna, which is camouflaged to look like a blade of grass. The receiver is set up beside the four claymore detonation devices and monitored by the man on watch, who also monitors the radio. An enemy soldier crossing the perimeter, no matter how quiet, sends shockwaves through the ground activating the seismic sensors. The guy on radio watch then wakes the team leader, apprising him of the situation—say, enemy approaching from the east—and he then decides whether to set off the eastern claymore and blow the bastard's nuts to smithereens. The sensors have five settings of sensitivity. At the

most sensitive even heavy rain might start them beep-
ing. An artillery shell landing close by or a thunder
clap could activate the sensors at any setting, so you
don't take chances and instead assume every beep is
Charlie creeping up.

You'd think a tropical jungle would be hot all
the time, but not in the northern highlands. During
the day you're dissolving in the heat. Your rucksack
feels like it's welded to your back. Then at night
the temperature can drop into the fifties, which you
might think is actually comfortable after the heat,
but it sure ain't when that rain never quits except just
long enough to let in a fog. And it gets worse when
trying to grab some sleep in a fighting hole half filled
with muddy water or even if laying on open ground.
There's no sense trying to stay dry. What difference
does it make keeping the rain off your head by drap-
ing a poncho over it when your ass is underwater?
So either you're about to melt in the heat or shiver
to death on cold wet nights made even colder when
a strong wind is blowing the rain around. The only
warmth is imaginary, coming from heat lightning
behind the clouds in the sky. Can't even bitch because
orders are to not move and to keep quiet. And hope
every creak of bamboo isn't telegraphing a band of
Viet Cong sneaking up to slit our throats. So you sit
there shivering in the wet dark and ast yourself over
and over, why the fuck am I here? For chrissakes I
ought to of joined up with the Air Force or some
other pussy branch of the service where they sleep

in real beds and eat hot food and don't have to hunt down and kill nobody or run the chance of getting their own ass killed off. I really, really don't need this shit. I don't.

The LT

The LT never wrote letters. There were no friends with whom to air his thoughts. He had no girlfriend or wife but appreciated how women smelled, like a strange candy not yet invented. It was something that seeped from their skin, a sweet secretion of exotic fructose. If indeed we are the composites of all experiences—past loves, friendships, antagonisms—he was incomplete, a developing embryo.

My dick is long and hard, its head calloused as a carpenter's thumb. It thinks thoughts of its own, desperate thoughts of slim brown thighs. We have long been victims of female pulchritude, my dick and I, stupefied by a shadowy feminine glow pulsating like a chameleon's chromatophores. There's no more beautiful sight than a slim ankle attached to a shapely calf, both riding atop a high-heeled shoe. Love, he knew from experience, is fleeting, the after-effects not so much. Unlike metal, which contracts as it cools, the molecular lattices of love expand and seek to distance themselves. One love in particular. He thought fiercely about her in the diminishing hours before her image departed with the light. There had always been lies, but more deafening were the unspoken omissions. And the fear. He was eternally sensitive to abuse from women, a blind reader of the post-ovulatory furies. Oh God, deliver me.

He put such thoughts aside and instead of correspondence he kept a notebook. It wasn't a diary or a journal in any sense because dates to him were irrelevant, yet he was obsessed with the notion of time in a theoretical sense, and especially with the ethereal *now*. He wrote in pencil because ink smudges and runs when wet, and often he wrote in fog and rain and near-darkness. He kept his notebook wrapped in plastic, but it wrinkled and warped nonetheless. He didn't care. The mental process preceding his entries mattered more than what was written. His notebook was thick, but could still fit in a pocket of his cammie trousers. It had a dull black cover on the inside of which he wrote his name. Just his name. He had no address worth remembering. When preparing to go on patrol the notebook was the first item he thought to bring.

On reading his notes later he was always reminded that he wasn't a warrior but maladroit thinker and a scribbler of sad sentences. This day he had written, "Love and war have this in common: in the absence of personal experience you can't possibly understand either."

The LT penciled notes about how it's possible to remain immobile in space but not in time, proof that time moves, or flows. How quickly does it move? At whatever rate you choose: one hour per hour, one minute per minute, one second per second. And at each rate the universe becomes an hour, a minute, a second older because the time generated is new.

What do we mean by every instant *is*? It occurred to him that everything we know or experience is imagined; nothing *is*, including the conceptual *now*, that immediacy of instantaneous events, even death. We can quantify the past using statistics and attempt to project the future with probability theory, but there is no reproducible way of describing and measuring *now*. So when is *now*? All time is *now*, just as it has been and will be. A *now* just went by to be replaced by another, and it too is *now*, further evidence of time's flow.

Using a different metaphor you could say that time flows around *now*, as a river parts and flows around an island. That the island appears to be immobile is attributable partly to our restricted concept of time. The metaphor works only if the island changes continuously, which it actually does. Invisible to the unaided eye a tiny sliver of earth from the island's edges washes away. A bird alights in a tree, in doing so dislodging a bit of bark. The bird swallows a bug, thus removing it. As the bird flies away it disturbs particles of dust on nearby leaves, rearranging them. A raindrop falls from the tree to the forest floor, dissolving a few atoms of rock and stimulating a nearby shrub to produce a new leaf. Its addition is how we define growth. Each event was an instantiation of *now*.

Nothing stays the same; a river can't be fixed in place because of an island in its center or by driving a stake into it. The date of an event—a singular collage of *nows* retained in memory—can be held immobile, but a date is a representation, the actual *now* or sequence of *nows* having passed into history.

How does the conceptual *now* work in everyday life? I just glanced at Hillbilly from five feet away. I thought, am I seeing you *now*? Of course not. That *now* already slipped through time like a cosmic eel. To complicate matters I see you as you were five-billionths of a second ago, the time it takes light to travel five feet. Add to this some time for the photons embedded in that "slice" of light to activate appropriate target cells of my visual pigments, form an upside-down image, and relay a signal containing the information to my brain. Factor in additional time for data contained in the signal to be analyzed and categorized as a face, then a little more for the image to be reconfigured rightside-up and sent to my facial recognition center in the fusiform gyrus. There an archive of memorized faces is opened for comparison of this image with all others. Tack on still more time while I decide I'm looking at you—Hillbilly—and not someone else. The face of you in my archive is clean-shaven, the face of a scared rookie. You were new in-country and new to our squad. You're not scared anymore, you're tired, hungry, and bug-bitten all to hell. This new image has a week-old beard and a smear of mud on the left cheek, but I still recognize it as you. Sum the time of these events to occur and it comes to far less than a millisecond.

The sequence from light reflecting off your face to recognition is so rapid and transparent it seems to occur without delay; that is, in "real" time. The process happens unconsciously and is part of epi-sodic memory; that is, within the realm of personal experience. Years later I might retrieve this visual image of your face, ageless and unshaven and dirty, and mistake it for a fragment of some departed *now*. Which it is, in a way. But a memory can't be *now*. It can only be a representation like this entry in my notebook that reads: "Another day added to the age of the universe. Another day when we didn't die."

Hillbilly

We took a break once under a big old tree and staged our gear against its trunk. Big ain't even the word. The sumbitch must've rose a hundred foot into the triple canopy and poked out above it. Back home it could of filled a regular forest by itself. Otherwise it looked like any tree, except to Bunny and Injun.

"Damn if this isn't a neem tree," Bunny said. He tilted back his head and looked skyward. "There's a specimen in the botanical garden, but it'll never in a million years grow this size." He stretched to full height, pulled down the lowest-hanging branch, and stripped off some of the leaves and pale yellow fruits and started to look them over. He said, "The fruit's edible, and juice from the seeds and inner bark is supposed to cure athlete's foot. They say if you chew the fresh seeds your gums won't get sore, and you keep your teeth."

"It's a good tree," Injun said. "I make a tea from the inner bark and drink it often as I can. Prevents malaria now that I ain't got Monday morning pills anymore. And I bet a poultice made out of the smushed seeds might help cure y'all's jungle rot." He and Bunny began picking the fruits and eating them. After a minute the rest of us did too, including the LT. We filled our pockets with seeds to chew while humping. What the hell, it couldn't hurt, and a guy needs to keep his teeth. They had a funny taste, but not too bad when I mixed them in with my chaw. I ast Injun where he got the bush coffee cup in his pocket, and he said, all around, y'all dropping them everywhere. It's like following along after the circus, he said, y'all leaving piles of shit wherever you go.

While we was setting around munching on fruit, Injun said, "Anyone who starves in the jungle is a certified dumbass. There's stuff to eat everywhere. It's a fucking banquet and a helluva lot better for you than any fucking C-rats. That shit will kill you. I always figured C-rats to be part of the Mother Green's plan. She's a cheap mother. If the bitch kills us off she can bring in new meat instead of promoting us to a higher pay grade." We regularly shot off our mouths like this, and the LT never said a word. He didn't seem to care either way, like he wasn't listening, just thinking about what to scribble next in his notebook.

Then he said, "Come see this." We gathered around, and he pointed to a bunch of ants marching along on the ground. We hadn't noticed them. "An ant colony is a little city of its own," he said. "It has workers and soldiers to protect the young and the food supply. The ants with the big heads and jaws are the soldiers. A soldier looks bizarre beside its fellow ants, the 'normal' ones scurrying around doing what ants do. Soldier ants are freaks. This one is us," he said. He picked up a soldier ant and looked at it closely. "A pissant with a big head and no brains. Get used to it.

"You don't need to be all that high in the air to see humankind as an anthill in need of exterminating. Just a couple of hundred feet will do. Go up in a helo and look down. Amazing how quickly sensibility switches mode. A little napalm here, a dash of Agent Orange over there for symmetry. . .you get the idea." He looked at us and smiled, and we laughed. The LT has a shallow smile, the kind that stops and follows until you look around suddenly and see that it's gone.

Bunny was loving the scene. He said he was start– ing to remember rainforest plants from the botanical garden more clearly, that their scientific names and uses were coming back. He said at first the jungle had washed over him like a tidal wave, same as it does everybody. The place is sure as hell intimidating with the strange noises and smells, the vegetation so big and close it seems to reach out for you. Nights in harbor are extra dark because it's usually raining or overcast and no moonlight filters down through the trees even in clear weather. It's scary with animal sounds and the wind making any nearby bamboo creak and moan. Usually it's raining to beat hell, and with raindrops the size of marbles hammering on the vegetation you can't hear shit. The VC travel mostly at night, so the thought of them sneaking up to the perimeter is always in your head. Day or night you're looking out for Charlie, venomous snakes, even tigers for chrissakes. Then there's the alternating heat and cold of the highlands, the constant wetness and jungle rot during monsoon, mosquitoes and flies. . . The danger and discomfort never end.

But as I say, Bunny was loving it. Now with Injun here he wants to taste everything, to learn everything Injun's learned during his time alone. For example, Injun has some what he calls "simple rules" about whether a plant you don't know nothing about might be safe to eat. That it might have medicinal value was a whole different matter. For that we'd need to ask the experts, he told us, he might be a Indian, but he ain't no goddamn medicine man. He was willing to vouch for the eating, nothing else. As most people know, in many cases only part of a plant might be edible, the leaves or stems, for example, or maybe the flowers, but not the fruit. Or vice versa. Sometimes a fruit is edible but its seeds can poison you.

Rule one: Never, *ever*, eat a mushroom unless you know exactly what the hell you're doing. Rule two: Don't eat roots and bulbs unless you know what the hell you're doing. Rule three: Don't eat plants that bleed white sap when you cut them, have green or white berries, thorny stems, or pods like string beans. Rule four: Don't eat leaves or stems that are hairy, scratchy, or prickly.

If you've made it to here and, say, decide to try a fruit you ain't tried before, break the skin first and rub the juice sort of light against your lips. If after

a minute your lips sting or feel numb, toss the fruit.
If it passes this test take a tiny bite and hold it in
your mouth for several minutes. If the taste is really
sour or unpleasant, or if there's a burning or stinging
sensation, spit it out and move on. If it don't sting or
hurt, take a bite and chew it a minute or so, but don't
swaller it. If you're still okay take a bite and swaller it.
Finally, whether you reject a plant or reckon to eat
part of it memorize what it looks like so you don't
have to repeat this process.

After Injun told us it was okay we ate a bunch
of reddish sweet-and-sour pods from a tree we
passed, Bunny called it a guamuchil. They're safe
even though they look like pea pods. Bunny said he
must of humped past a hundred of these trees while
out on patrol and their identity never clicked. He
remembered from a label at the botanical garden that
a tea brewed from the root bark could cure chronic
dysentery. Man, our ears perked up on hearing that.
Nothing is more aggravating than a sweaty case of
ass and crotch rot combined with the shits. Every step
is like sandpaper rubbing between your butt cheeks.
You get so you can barely walk. We dug around the
base with our E-tools and scraped together a pile of
root bark. We rinsed it off, filled our boonie cups
with canteen water, and boiled some of that bark on
the spot until the liquid turned brown. Goddamn if
it didn't start to work after a couple of days. Our ass
rot didn't go away, but at least the shits did. A jarhead
without the feeling of a hot poker up his asshole is a

happier jarhead, guaran–damn–teed. Amazing what a little comfort does for the attitude.

Hillbilly Again

One time the LT ast me about my name, and I told him I was named by my mama after a song on a record. He said it was strange but not unheard of, someone being named after a song. After all, he said, people can be named after months of the year, even days of the week, that he once knowed a boy named Thursday. He ast me where I come from, and I said Scalded Creek. I told him it's a coal camp in West Virginia down near the border with the state of Kentucky, and I mentioned I was once in Kentucky and didn't even know, it looked the same as where I'd just crossed over. Even the clouds in the sky was the same, the birdsongs, the leaves on the trees. . .everything, that one place is pretty much the same as another. Not here, though, where nothing is the same as anywhere excepting maybe Hell.

He ast if I had kin, and I said none I knowed of above ground, and he said it was the same with him and that when he was gone his line went with him into oblivion. He told me he come from Mississippi, but in the middle part, not the delta, although they still growed cotton where he lived, and not down in the south beside the ocean nor in the northern parts that look like Tennessee. I said I'd never been to any of them places.

I ast him, "Sir, does wearing a flak jacket make any difference?" He told me it did, but whether you lived or died depended on how close you was to the blast and lots of other things. I ast him if I'd be twice as safe if I wore two, one atop the other.

He looked off into the jungle like he does when he's thinking stuff, then he turned back to me and said, "No, it won't. But the real answer is complicated, and I thank you for bringing it up because I need to do some figuring and then give a little talk to the men when we get back to base." Nobody had ever said thank you to me for anything, and him saying it made me real proud.

I didn't feel uncomfortable walking up to the LT and talking to him even though he's an officer. He's real nice and speaks to you soft, but he expects us to jump when he tells us to. Before monsoon season we was patrolling the valleys. There warn't any action, so one evening after we made harbor and set the perimeter I ast him if he'd help me write a letter to my girl Twyla Ray. I said I wasn't much for reading and writing, that back home we didn't put much stock in schooling, and I'd never wrote a letter except the ones they made us write in boot to say we was okay and loved life in the Corps. Boot, where they run us hard and made us sweat and scramble over log barriers no harder to climb than treefalls in squirrel season. I sent my letters to Mama and Daddy, but they never wrote me back. I didn't expect them too. Anyway the LT said, sure, I'll help you. Let's set down here under this tree. I'll get out my notebook. You tell me what you want to say and I'll jot it down. So I did. I ast Twyla Ray to say hidey to my folks and a few of the guys I used to pal around with. I told the LT about some of the miners in the camp who are younger than Daddy but older than me. Daddy was in the Army in the Second World War. These other guys went to Korea, and now here I am in Vietnam. I give him some names, which he wrote down. It was a short letter. I still keep the LT's copy of this one in my pocket. We wrote some others, but they got all soggy in the wetness and I throwed them out eventually. The first letter said:

Hi there, Twyla Ray

Hope you are well. I am over here in Vietnam where the weather is hot. We have not fought the enemy but hope to soon. We go out on patrol sometimes and sleep in the jungle, and that is dangerous. Say hidey to my folks and any of my buddies you see hanging around. Also to Thaddeus, Thrice, Owner, Old Ed, and Randi Sue over at the Smokehouse Grill.

Yours sincerely,
Danny Boy Beaver

103

After the LT had wrote down my words he tore the page out of his notebook, folded it up, and handed it to me. He told me when we got back to base to copy what was wrote onto a new piece of paper in my own handwriting. He said he'd give me a stamped envelope so's I could mail it off. I reckon Twyla Ray got that letter and the others, but if she did she never wrote me back that I know of. We wrote her five, maybe six letters, me and the LT. In some we told her about the guys on the fireteam, how we was like brothers. We described everyone except the LT hisself who said he didn't think he ought to be part of the story. Twyla Ray's probably the same as me and never wrote a letter by herself. I can't remember how long it's been since I sent them off, but probably a couple of months.

Sometimes when we took a break on patrol I'd tell the LT about the people I named in them letters. I didn't tell him about some others back home I'm familiar with and decided not to mention either to him or on paper. I got my own reasons, which the LT don't need to hear or know about. It's personal. Some people, they're assholes, if you get what I mean. The LT had heard me talk about Scalded Creek before, but after the letters him and me wrote together they now seemed like his friends too. He told me he felt he practically knowed them right down to their shoe sizes and what each one looked like and what brand of beer they drank. It made me feel good.

The LT can be a little weird. I've watched him

hold up a tiny mirror and aim his flashlight at it. He opens his mouth and looks deep into his gullet, making gagging sounds as he tries to flatten the back of his tongue, I guess to look even deeper. I wonder what he sees and whether he wonders too. What's he hunting for? Maybe he's found it already and just needs something to write down in his notebook.

The LT

I'm always asked about flak jackets by the grunts, who don't like wearing them but still worry about getting wounded or killed by shrapnel. This notebook entry is for when we get back to base. I'll muster the squad and give them a little talk. I'll say that a flak jacket is indeed heavy and hot. It restricts movement, slows you down, forces you to hump harder and tire sooner. Is wearing it worthwhile? Will just one be sufficient or do I need to layer them? What if I wear two?

Assume that one absorbs half the flak (merely an assumption), leaving "only" the remaining fifty percent to maim or kill its wearer. If you thought wearing two makes you doubly safe you'd be wrong. Layering one atop another would absorb seventy-five percent of the shrapnel, not twice as much. On the bright side there would theoretically still be twenty-five percent less shrapnel hitting me than if I had been wearing just one. Of course, less than a fraction of one percent can be lethal. A tiny piece so small as to be barely visible can kill instantly or even after many years if it shifts to a crucial location inside the body.

If I wear three jackets? Three would absorb eighty-seven and a half percent. And four? (Has anyone ever worn four?) You'd look like a kid bundled in multiple snowsuits and in this heat know the feeling of slow cremation, but the potential flak absorbed would rise to ninety-three and three-fourths percent. Can one hundred percent protection from shrapnel ever be attained by layering flak jackets? Only by never being hit.

Hillbilly

During down time at base lots of the guys laid around talking about their families, but not so much our fireteam. The LT don't seem to have one. Bunny has just his mom, Poke has his pa and little sister plus their hired man Jorge who's practically a member of the family. And if you was to ast Poke he'd likely tell you not to leave out Spooky, his horse. Injun? Who knows? I recall him naming his ma and pa maybe once, but we ain't heard about no brothers and sisters.

In my case we was never much of what you'd call a close family where people admire one another and get along. Daddy was mostly in the mines working shift, and when he warn't working or sleeping he drank, whiskey and beer mostly, but moonshine too if it was any good. Mama was always tired and complaining about the coal dust everywhere, that she couldn't even keep doilies on the chair arms because they just turned black. She seemed to cry a lot. Nobody ever mentioned if I had any aunts and uncles and maybe some cousins too. My grandparents, they're dead.

I'm the only kid if you don't count the one that died. There had been a stillborn brother who come along after me, and when I was younger I used to wonder how a soul that small could claw its way out of a wooden box and then through all that packed earth before being free enough to fly to Heaven. He'd been just a fetus with fingernails scarcely formed and still soft. Mama had just gived birth. The granny woman was still there in the house, and her and Daddy and me was gathered around the kitchen table where the baby was laid out on a towel. He looked like a little girl's doll except more wrinkled. I remember the tiny dead fingers partly extended as if in the middle of grasping for something, maybe the hand of his older brother, reaching out for his brother's grubby fingers with their nails already hardened and blackened and split. Our parents was going to name him Esaw, but he went into the ground unnamed because Daddy said that before you could have a name you had to draw a breath; you had to be "in the world." And so the tombstone just said "Baby Beaver" with a single date. He might of been a frog or a sparrow.

Daddy never liked me and didn't tried to hide it. When I was little he used to say, "A kid ain't nothing but a shit sandwich, and every morning of my life is another bite." He said that after a hard day's work a man just wanted to be left alone, and he'd yell at Mama to keep me away from him. Nothing changed much as the years went by, so I figured to help him out by leaving. The day after I turned eighteen I joined up with the Corps. Me and three buddies went over to the recruiting office in Logan, showed our drivers licenses, got swore in, and signed the papers. And then we went out and drunk a beer to celebrate.

When I got home and told the parents Mama went and set at the kitchen table and cried. Daddy didn't say nothing at first, but didn't seem surprised. Him and me was standing in the living room looking at one another. Finally he put a hand to my chest and pushed me down on the couch. Then he went to the kitchen and poured hisself a glass of whiskey and come and set in the armchair acrost the room. His chair, he called it. Mama and me knowed never to set in it.

"I got some advice," Daddy said, "so listen up. I didn't come out of the Great War against Hitler and his krauts without learning a few things, stuff you need to know. And I learned things from your papa who was in World War I and who's dead now, God rest his soul. They called his war the Great War too, but war is war. It don't matter when or where or which one you're in. Any of them sounds 'great' until you find yourself ass-deep in it.

"In the military you'll meet all kinds: reverends, murderers, liars, thieves, drunks, dope addicts, even homosexuals. Don't judge nobody else, and never pass up a opportunity to keep your mouth shut. Expect to come home dead, but if you survive it'll be 'cause you're lucky or stayed amongst the herd in times of combat. There ain't a helluva lot of difference between heroes and fools. Both tend to go off by theirself and do something stupid. That'll either get you a medal, a pine box, or both, so don't be neither. What I'm telling you is keep your head down, your butt cheeks squeezed tight, and your pecker in your pants. Got it?"

The last time I seed Mama and Daddy was the morning I left on the bus for Parris Island. When I said goodbye to Mama she was setting at the kitchen table crying. She spent a lot of time beside that table crying for one reason or another. She told me Daddy was down at the Smokehouse Grill, so I went there before walking out to stand beside the hard road to wait on the bus. Did Daddy ever really love us? I ast myself this question a hundred times and never come up with any answer. Truth is, I don't know.

I went into the Smokehouse and said goodbye to the regulars and to Randi Sue tending bar. It was ten or so of the morning. Daddy had just retired from mining, and when I went to shake his hand he never took his eyes off Thaddeus setting beside him and waved me away like he would a bug, a bothersome gnat in a corner of his bloodshot eye.

Him and Thaddeus was deep into one of their important discussions, and Daddy was saying, "You ain't old 'til you take yourself out of life's events, when you get to where you really don't care no longer. Take the miner's union. You always paid your dues and went to the meetings. You listened to the speeches and tried your damnedest to separate the truth from the horseshit. Then one morning you wake up, put your feet on the floor same as always. The sun has came up and the rooster crowed, like always. You ain't especially angry or perturbed, you just don't give a shit anymore. It's simple as that, it really is. Now, would you kindly reach me that salt shaker? This beer I'm looking at is painfully shy on bubbles."

We did have one more short discussion before I went away, me and him. He told me, "The military's like God, hell-bent on killing you to no decent purpose."

I said, "But the recruiter told us war's the only real thing, Daddy."

"No, sonny boy," he said, "the only real thing is this here holler and the food I put on the table, and maybe pussy without which there'd be no humankind."

After the bus pulled away I never laid eyes on him and Mama again. Just as I was finishing up boot I got word they'd got killed in a car crash someplace there in Logan County. They never went anywhere together in the car, but he was just retired, so Lord knows what they was up to.

The news come in a telegram our platoon leader give me. I remember I was setting on my cot working at my boots, and I put them aside along with the polishing gear so's to read the message. The Marines would of excused me for the funeral, but I didn't want to go anyway. Wouldn't of made a difference 'cause their death didn't affect me one way or the other. Call it strange, but I didn't feel nothing emotional. They was dead, and that was that. Guess they was buried there in the camp. We got a churchyard in Scalded Creek where they bury dead folks, but I can't say for sure if that's where they are. Reckon I'll hear about it when I get home someday. I kept the telegram. Couldn't tell you why.

The LT

His first tour of Vietnam had been, in a way, a revelation because the experience had taught him little. The firefights had been unnerving and frightening, forcing him to think about time and mortality, but he nonetheless emerged puzzled at how little he changed. He had expected to have emerged wiser, more appreciative of what being alive means, enthusiastic about the future. He felt none of these transformations.

He was due leave and then reassignment, so he went to Saigon for a few days of R & R and checked into a hotel. The lobby was jammed with military personnel on leave, with journalists, hookers, civilian contractors, and government gnomes scurrying through sweating and toting briefcases.

After signing the ledger and being handed a room key in he spent the rest of the first day lying in bed smoking and looking at the ceiling, vaguely aware of his body heat dissipating into the air-conditioned space and increasing its entropy. It seemed backward to think of a war zone as a place of thermal order and Saigon as disorderly. At nightfall he showered, changed into civvies, and went down to the dining room. After dinner, and wearing a slight buzz from two bourbons on the rocks and a bottle of wine, he bought an overpriced nickel bag of weed and a packet of rolling papers from the elevator operator and returned to his room on the fourth floor. He stripped to his skivvies, shut off the air-conditioning, and opened the window, and as noise from the streets filtered up, got stoned. In the morning he awoke wondering momentarily where he was. The room was stifling. He felt as he'd spent the night in a sauna; the sheets were wet with his sweat and reeking of fear from dreams now dissipated.

During the next few days he walked along sidewalks buckled by the roots of ancient trees, their upper parts deformed and leaning, crippled by lightning. In a section where the sidewalks had been repaired with new cement children had left tiny footprints as might a herd of prehistoric animals passing across an ancient mudflat. Narrow alleys snaked between the streets slick and wet after a rain, smelling of spices and of picked vegetables too long in the sun. The open-air markets sold Snickers bars and blonde Caucasian dolls dressed as cheerleaders that closed their china-blue eyes when tipped back. Trash bins made of pre-formed plastic in the shape of open-mouthed penguins begged to receive American refuse. What is it about America's insolent postmodernism, he wondered, that other cultures find so attractive, even those we're attempting to stamp out? But only in the cities. We bomb the rural countryside into wasteland, turning graveyards of the ancestors into dust until not even their ghosts remain.

At night the streets of Saigon hummed with whispered confessions. Whispers, he knew, are more than exhaled air, and they bear more weight than might be imagined. Neon signs advertised liquor and sex shows featuring underage girls. Mini-skirted hookers beckoned from doorways. In his musings it occurred to him how the purpose of science is to trivialize nature by making its mysteries explicit, and that pornography does the same for sex.

He avoided other Americans, feeling he had nothing relevant to say, nor they to him. Discussions were always about postings, duration in-country, time remaining until rollover back to the World, and family. He didn't have any family, and the rest he considered mundane: his experiences were qualitatively no different from those of many others like himself. Viewed this way, what was there to talk about?

On the next to last night of his stay he drank more than usual at a dingy place several blocks from his hotel and picked up a bar girl. He chose her because she behaved less aggressively than the others, who went from man to man until finding one willing to pay. Her eyes were thick with makeup, something green and sparkly with a heavy atomic weight.

They negotiated a price and walked around the corner to a shabby hotel. The clerk handed her the key to a room down a dark hall where she unlocked the door. He wondered briefly if the door could be booby-trapped, then realized he was getting paranoid. A door, he reminded himself, consists of molecules of wood rearranged to suit a purpose, fulfill a function. Our own are not different, and both a door and the man who uses it eventually are reduced to bare elements without shape awaiting rearrangement into something else tangible: a leaf, a dung beetle, a drop of water. He stepped across the threshold finding his own arrangement of molecules still intact.

They had indifferent sex atop a rumpled mattress on the floor. She got up afterward and turned on a table lamp. Her casual attitude toward nakedness seemed natural, which struck him as an unusual attribute between strangers, considering humans have been wearing clothes of one sort of another for thousands of years. Then she returned and sat beside him. His clothes were hanging on a nearby chair. Without getting up he rummaged in his pants pockets and produced a joint. They smoked it, then another. Thoroughly stoned, he looked at her, wondering if he could ever get off the mattress and stand long enough to dress and leave.

In the past—before the war, that is—he had always withheld himself, giving to others the appearance of lacking empathy. He remained impervious to their wishes and entreaties, his being devoid of those porous features into which another's humanity was permitted to seep.

She watched him impassively, and suddenly he

was swamped by feelings of generosity and tenderness. Unexpectedly he blurted out that he wanted
to protect her, but the words came back delayed
and false, like distant echoes. He felt an urge to
explain everything, how war is the most primitive
of human pursuits because it existed in our hearts
before recorded time.

She started to weep, her throat making little
huffing noises, tiny hands pressed like open fans over-
lapping her face. "Me? But I just a whore!" The drapes
on the single window were spongy-looking and the
color of coagulated blood. Light from a street lamp
poured through broken slats in the blinds giving her
the striped appearance of a prisoner trapped behind
bars. It was happening, he thought, a moment when
the ceilings of my own dreams press down and the
world of make-believe darkens and I awake suddenly
to see myself clambering over the rubble of a ruined
city. I hear the screams of the dying, but they sound
like reverberations inside my head, like an intermit-
tent series of faint rasps. That and my own heartbeats.

"We're all whores, here in this place," he said.

The night hummed, and he fell in with its har-
mony. Moths fluttered around the paltry glow of the
lamp, their wings making tiny thumping sounds as
they struck the interior of the shade. Ching-chongy
music backing a tentative vocalist singing in Vietnamese filtered in from outside and rolled around in
his brain like a marble clanging off the ridges and
troughs of a roulette wheel. For a second he thought

of himself as a warbler dying without having sung his own song.

The room had no mirror, but in his stupor he imagined a creeping kinesis fronted by a sorry reflection of himself in the depressing present. An unknown voice whispered regretfully inside his head. It was a voice of authority telling him nobody controls the big stuff—the war and its unpredictability—so instead we higher-highers deify our shitty little regulations, issuing more each day as the fear and uncertainty creep closer. Marine commanders abhor the asymmetrical. But his brain was warning him once again that whispers are more than the air we breathe out, and they bear more weight than can be imagined.

He felt spent and disposable. I've become like an old flashlight battery, he thought, losing function. I've shined too brightly for too long and after the weeks and months in service my performance is in steady decline. Ahead could only be a concomitant and inevitable loss of autonomy and final capitulation to the Corps' insatiable engine. In its final throes a battery demonstrates rising internal resistance, decaying voltage, ultimate loss of energy, and finally death.

He considered crawling toward the door and hiding behind it, moving slowly so as not to alert the eyes of the predator. Oh, here I come! He laughed falsely at the girl, his sweaty skin about to make contact with the heat of the night. He thought, what if fog subtracts from the sky instead of adding to it? In this brittle new clarity I might see a familiar woman arise out of memory's ashes. What if she beckons to me and I follow? What then?

The next morning he slept late and in the afternoon found Marine headquarters and arranged not to be rotated back to the States but assigned again to his old company. He realized he'd come to admire the spit-shines and simple order, the high-and-tight haircuts and the culture of elbows and assholes, even the brainless jargon and rampant ignorance. Until the war ended he could squint at the sky and postpone his dreams, presently narrow and unfinished anyway. And what then? Which is more cruel when the zoo closes for good: to free the lion into an unfamiliar landscape where death is certain but freedom at least fleeting, or to shoot him in his cage?

Nature is proof enough that something is larger than one man's self-pity. The jungle was a marvel with its savage life all around, its relentless heat and vegetable fecundity. In solitude he could hear it chewing, swallowing, consuming. And still it grew until the U.S. military came along and painted it a brittle dead-brown with Agent Orange and slowing, if only temporarily, the growth of that which was chewed and swallowed.

The end was inevitable, the choices few. The Marines shipped you home eventually, dead or alive or somewhere in between, if not in a box then still breathing perhaps with a substantially useful body part missing. Of course there were those cases when nothing at all came home. Then it could be surmised that an unknown winged creature—and angel or maybe a vulture—had fetched you somewhere heavenly, or not.

He had become nearly indifferent to what went on around him, partly because the fires inside his mind were brighter than the dull embers outside. He had no wish to revisit the confident, shining illusion of America, not when he could stay here. Vietnam was its own manifestation of unreality, a place of scuttling shadows, of sorrows wearing pointed hats made from palm leaves, of false light and real darkness.

The LT Again

As soon as Injun appeared behind us and we'd gotten over our surprise I figured we ought to regroup and get our shit together. After talking with the base Actual of Injun's platoon I asked Injun for a situation report. He said the area was clear of enemy activity, that he hadn't come across evidence of VC in days. Then I wanted to know the "friendly situation"; in other words, whether another U.S. military unit might be operating nearby and if so what its radio frequency and call sign were in case we needed to make contact. "Negative on that too, sir," Injun said, admitting he wouldn't have contact information after having been on his own so long. I said I knew as much, but had he found evidence of friendlies in the area recently? Injun stood before me uninhibited in raw, savage elegance, posing in his rippling muscles like an anatomical dissection. By acknowledging my authority at least his military discipline seemed to have remained unperturbed. Or so I thought, until he added, "Nobody here but us chickens, uh, sir."

I knew the men were looking at one another

wondering what my response might be, but I let it go. I really like these guys, all of them. We refer to them as men, but most are kids still in their teens. We put them through hell, and they handle it, most of them gracefully, some with humor, and a few even with irony. How many their age at home are forced to think about the possibility of death every day and try to guess who's next to be sent back to their families in a glad bag?

We took a break under a specimen of the tree Bunny and Injun had identified earlier, which we all now recognized. After eating some of its fruit and taking a smoke we saddled up. I assigned Injun to walk point after first reviewing our hand signals with him and everyone else: freeze (closed fist against to the chest), freeze and listen (closed fist held to the face with index finger against the ear), and so forth.

On the "freeze" signal we kneel instantly and orient toward our designated "area of responsibility." For the point man this means maintain eyes to the front and scan an area of one-hundred-eighty degrees. The second man points his rifle right and scans the scene. The third points his left, and so on down the line, right, left, right, left, or in Marine jargon, "inboard-outboard." Tail-end Charlie, the last member of the team, covers the rear and scans one hundred-eighty degrees behind us. When on the hump and terrain permitting, tail-end Charlie walked backward.

Christ, he took to it like a beagle. He said it was

okay to be a little casual, that the area really was clear. Based on what the base Actual had said I decided to give him his head but stay close until I could read him better. To do so I shifted forward one place to second in the order. If we engaged any VC I'd have to move quickly to point because Injun didn't have a weapon. It felt like the Old West, an Indian scout leading and the troops falling in line behind him.

We were leaving the highlands temporarily. Our orders were to check out a ville in the valley below that was rumored to be a VC staging area. Recon intel suspected the villagers themselves were VC, or at least VC sympathizers, which meant a potentially "hot" situation with expectation of direct engagement. When I showed Injun the map he waved it away. He knew the location, having reconnoitered it previously with his team, and had even sneaked into the ville at night and looked around. At the time, he said, it sheltered an unusually large stash of rice stored in earthenware jars, more than a single village would need to survive after the harvest. Someone else was obviously benefiting. Recon's mission was to search and collect intelligence, ours to follow up and destroy. Onset of the monsoon season had delayed the destroy aspect by weeks, meaning we might get there and find nothing. Our instructions were straightforward: roust the villagers, search the premises for VC, and burn their food supplies. After accomplishing the mission, radio base for evac.

The trail switch-backed across the mountainside

for several klicks, becoming at times nearly vertical. Progress was often slowed to a near standstill by treefalls, curtains of lianas, and man-high stands of vegetation with leaves the size of tabletops. In places the path metamorphosed into a stream of mud and water. We slipped and slid continuously, often falling and bumping into each other. There was the usual muttering and cursing and yips of pain as thorns penetrated arms and legs or someone's knee encountered a sharp rock. Injun didn't hump anything except himself, but was there to temporarily grab a weapon or hold a pack strap when one of us needed two hands to keep from tumbling out of sight into the green maw below.

As the terrain leveled out Injun whispered to me it was time to go on alert, and I passed the word along. At the bottom of the mountain we stopped to listen and catch our breath. The day was fading, and the ville was still a long hump west toward Laos. At least another full day and part of the next. We trekked silently into the rainforest and picked out a harbor site.

The night was uneventful, the best kind. Another day gone by without casualties, another notch in the time-left stick if you're keeping one. Still no sign of Charlie, no word from base, meaning our instructions still held: check out aforesaid ville and poke through it for recent VC activity. Burn any food stores; when mission accomplished, call in a bird for evac. We've been gone seven days, time enough in the bush for the guys to need a breather from the discomfort and tension. Only Injun and I have seen action in this war, and I'd like to keep it that way. I want to see my guys happy and healthy and back in the World.

Whether Injun comes along when we're evac'd is problematic, considering he'll be subjected to punishment of some kind as soon as the higher-highers lay hands on him. At the least, time in the brig. I wouldn't be surprised if he simply walks away before the chopper arrives. The rules he violated classify him as a disciplinary problem, which is too bad. I think he's a helluva Marine and would welcome him on my team anytime just as he is. Who the fuck cares if he's eccentric?

After the usual routine of cleaning weapons, eating breakfast, dismantling perimeter security, and checking the map and compass readings a final time, we pack our gear and prepare to move out. Most of the guys bring along some form of personal entertainment when on patrol. It lets them forget the war, if only intermittently and for a few minutes.

Everyone's diversion is different. I carry a notebook filled with useless scribblings to which I'm always adding more. Maybe I'll dig through it someday and write a war memoir, although I doubt it. The recounting of anyone's life is futile considering none of us has ever lived. A person's life is a diary without dates or palpable chronology. If I tell my story it will be a factless autobiography similar to Fernando Pessoa's *The Book of Disquiet*, recollections in which events are ethereal memories and dates of birth and death, like everything else, simply arbitrary impositions. Such a story accurately recounts the life of a man such as I who never existed. No matter. The world has enough war memoirs, and underneath they all have a common theme: war is hell, good people are killed and wounded, and you had to experience events personally to understand war's true essence. Because I get all this I don't see anything original I could contribute. What would be achieved by telling my story? Surely a critic who had never been to war would label it beyond belief, and one who had would peg it not realistic enough. Everyone has a different vision of what a war ought to be, a different memory of how it actually was, a uniquely personal vision of Hell. The itch you feel or the searing pain—it makes no difference—it can only be your own.

Writing a book is just a trick to influence strangers. My aspiration is much more modest: to write a single sentence of such truth and power that it rakes the gravel off hillsides like a M777 howitzer, explodes out my ears, causes snow to melt, and induces women to spread their legs. I can't see any of that happening.

The rest of the guys? Bunny humps a field guide to the plants of southeast Asia, a hardback that adds at least two pounds to his rucksack, equivalent to two M61 fragmentation grenades. The pages are dog-eared, the margins filled with penciled notes supplementing and updating the botanical descriptions. He's forever plucking a flower when we take a break and examining it under his jeweler's loupe, which magnifies objects ten times. He tells me that in botany the flowering part of a plant contains the most complete diagnostic clues to its identity, and he thinks there's nothing more exciting than counting the stamens or some other floral structures and finding a mistake in the guide, which he then corrects. Hillbilly totes a portable tape player of shit-kicker music he listens to whenever we're in a safe zone. Some guys hump girlie mags, but not Poke. His reading material comprises catalogues. I've seen him leafing through one that lists brands of lariats used for calf roping and another from the Oliver Saddle Shop in Amarillo. And he reads and re-reads an article torn from a magazine on how to train a roping horse. The pages are so grubby from use they're scarcely legible, but Poke probably has the content memorized, so it doesn't matter. Injun doesn't carry anything personal. His lifestyle is apparently diversion enough.

The forest was starting to thin as we moved nearer to the valley floor, no longer three-tiered and quite so gloomy. The rain had attenuated to a heavy, soaking mist, although visibility was still poor. Injun passed back word to come alive, that he was detecting signs of recent activity, whether the enemy or just locals foraging for wild plants and firewood he couldn't yet tell. We had humped maybe three klicks since daybreak, welcoming the easier going, when Injun gave the halt sign. He paused a moment while looking at the ground, then waved us to join him.

Beside the trail lay the rotting remains of an NVA infantry soldier, identifiable by remnants of his uniform: khaki shirt and trousers, a few distinguishing buttons, and placement of the pockets. Soon he would vanish under encroaching vegetation, the mud having already stained his bones and camouflaged them. Death is degrading for many reasons, but mainly because it shortens your stature. You lie there with everything and everyone above you, vulnerable suddenly to worms and beetles, fallen leaves and the creep of grass.

Liquid nutrients released from the decomposing flesh had collected around the corpse, fertilizing the impoverished soil. A continuous rim of small white mushrooms now lined its edges, reminiscent of the chalk outlines detectives draw around murder victims. Injun stuffed his pockets with several handfuls and began eating them as we continued. Bunny picked one and ate it, then looked at me and shrugged. "Crazy fuckers," Hillbilly said quietly, almost reverently.

Walking directly behind Injun was a revelation. After finding the corpse our pace had slowed considerably because Injun began dropping to all fours every few meters and sniffing the trail. The human sense of smell is acute, needing only training and practice to blossom fully, a talent Injun had developed while growing up in the Everglades. Tracking and wringing information from the environment were ingrained in him. He motioned me to him without taking his eyes off whatever he was looking at nearby.

I crept up and squatted beside him.

"See this?" He pointed to a faint impression in the soil. "A Charlie wearing sandals made out of old tires." I looked but couldn't make out the faint ridges and depressions he was outlining in the air with an index finger. He kneeled down and sniffed. "Probably yesterday morning, but hard to tell with the rain. Lots easier to pin down a time in the dry season."

We moved on, Injun's head swiveling, watching the trail ahead for trip wires and the surrounding vegetation for a disturbance or strange scent. He dropped to the ground frequently now, sniffing places alternately with one nostril then the other. I'd watched military dogs track, and they seemed to do the same thing, sniffing in odors through first one nostril then the other, perhaps giving the target receptors an opportunity to average data between the two and refine the assessment. At one place Injun stepped into the forest and was gone several minutes. The rest of us waited silently. When he returned we gathered in a tight group, and he whispered that a VC had taken a shit, probably yesterday.

"How do you know he was VC and not a local?" I said.

"From what he'd been eating. Reconstituted dried fish with cabbage. The food a VC carries leaves a distinct odor. Every person also has a personal body odor different from anyone else's. I'd recognize each of y'all in the dark by your scent, and I'd recognize him again too."

131

The Event

The land was heavily booby-trapped, and it took them all day to hump slightly more than ten klicks over mostly easy ground. In late afternoon, well before dusk, the LT ordered a halt and with Injun's assistance started searching for a harbor site. After finding one a perimeter was carefully set. The LT declined even to clear a field of fire, fearing the underbrush might conceal mines or IEDs. They remained on high alert through a claustrophobic night of intense blackness during which the land and sky were occluded by heavy mist. The wind had died completely. Not a whisper of a breeze stirred the vegetation, adding a measure of safety against an enemy creeping toward the perimeter, but also heightening anxiety: every drop of water rolling off a leaf and striking the one below fractured the quiet. The men waited uneasily for any stirring or disruption in the pattern of drips that could signal an impending attack.

But the night was uneventful, and day dawned bright and clear portending good weather. It was the first morning in weeks without rain, and the men's spirits rose. After saddling up and moving out they were smiling and joking. Only a few more klicks to the ville through what had become nearly open country. In such terrain a patrol customarily spreads out and advances in a horizontal line, but the LT, more wary of hidden ordnance than ambushes, kept everyone single file as if they were still walking jungle trails. A brief shower passed through, lasting just long enough to roust mosquitoes out of the grass and from around the rims of tiny vernal pools that were actually craters made by artillery shells. They were walking through air the density of cotton. The sun rose higher subsuming their humanity in the heat haze and transforming them into rippling mirages of legless torsos.

Much of the valley floor was under cultivation, although the paddies and fields were deserted. Where was everyone? The countryside looked tired and lived in, crisscrossed by invisible highways still trodden by livestock and by pilgrims seeking out their mute gods. The situation was unnerving in a different way from the previous night when there had been no visibility at all. The land, now an open vista, seemed to be observing them as if peopled by ghost farmers who stood in guarded silence and leaned on their hoes as they passed. Birds flitted between distant trees trailing remnants of song, but otherwise the air was still; they heard only the creak and crunch made by their boots and the airy sounds of their own breathing. Elephant grass in thick stands occasionally blocked the way, and all except Injun cursed its biting edges.

Injun stopped briefly to show them that the newly emergent leaves and stems are edible.

They passed carefully tended patches of sweet potatoes, and Injun stopped to pick and eat handfuls of the leaves. Farther on were isolated gardens of squashes in bloom. Injun, after showing that the flowers were edible, filled his pockets. He told them he occasionally left the mountains and moved through the valleys, covertly following village women as they foraged. From them he learned the identities and names of edible plants. He could creep near enough undetected to hear their conversations and see them pointing to plants or their parts before picking them. They call squash blossoms *bông bí*, he said. In a stand of bananas he demonstrated that not just the fruit is edible, so is its flower (*hoa chuôi*). And when nights were filled with the scent of jasmine, Injun often tracked down the source because the buds and blossoms, called by the women *bông thiên lý*, made a tasty snack.

They continued through the countryside circumventing isolated trip wires, still seeing no signs of life. Injun, despite his months in-country, could provide no explanation for the seeming absence of human life. He told everyone to be extra careful where they stepped from now on because there were booby traps all around. And once inside the ville no one was to open a gate or door of any kind without careful inspection. Anything with a moving part could be wired to yank the pin of a grenade or trip an IED.

They stopped for lunch beside a large stand of elephant grass, the ville not more than a klick or so away. Patches of lumpy white clouds floated above like batting from a newly eviscerated quilt. The LT was uneasy, feeling as if pursued by emptiness, of being trapped in a small space where existence takes the appearance of a rabid dog and escape is impossible. He felt like abandoning the mission and calling for evac, but could not think of an excuse. A premonition? Not reason enough. The men were in good spirits, knowing the patrol was nearly at an end. Injun, however, had suddenly become impassive and aloof, which the LT attributed to his impending departure.

When they once again saddled up, Injun came along, still part of the team and evidently intending to stick with them through completion of the mission before vanishing into the landscape. The location of the ville was now in sight, a tiny world closed in on itself. They traipsed single file along a dike covered by grass cropped close by geese, no longer wary of booby traps. The paddies surrounding the village were occupied by several untended water buffaloes submerged to their bellies. From the water's edge a wading bird looked up at them, unafraid. Insects buzzed in the oppressive air. A leaden breeze rose suddenly, pushing the surface of the paddies into silvery ripples that fled back and forth as if driven by shoals of frantic minnows.

They crossed the dike, locked and loaded. The village was surrounded by a nearly impenetrable wall

of green and yellow bamboo twenty feet tall. The
LT flashed the hand signal to disperse and search for
openings. The signal, along with verbal instructions,
had been given at the last stop. They were to stand
in place after each had discovered an opening and
wait for a signal to enter the ville simultaneously
from their different locations. Faint village sounds
filtered through the living barrier: ducks quack-
ing contentedly, the shuffling of sandaled feet, pigs
grunting, a child crying softly. . . Injun appeared at
his side. "They know we're here," he whispered. "I
smell their fear."

By now the LT trusted Injun's senses completely. "VC?"

"Not VC unless they're living here. I'd smell them,
but I don't. I can't smell that food Charlie carries
either, which I would if they were here for re-supply.
I only smell what farmers eat: rice cooked with eels
and other fish trapped in the paddies, garden vegetables. Shit like that. Nothing eaten on the move."

The LT gave the signal, which was passed along,
and they stepped in unison through the green wall.
Their appearance caused instantaneous pandemonium.
They had entered from several compass points and
arrived with rifles pointed at the huts, swinging them
from one adult to the next as the occupants ran screaming and unarmed into the open certain they would die.
The LT ordered his men to round everyone up and
confine them to an area several yards from the huts,
although well away from the bamboo and possible

escape. The women and girls represented a range of ages; the males were either old men, some hobbling on canes, or young boys. Perhaps those of military age had been conscripted by the ARVN or joined the VC guerrillas voluntarily. In any case the residents offered no resistance and did not appear dangerous.

The ville contained a dozen or so huts, all evidently occupied except one. Set apart from the others, it was probably used for storage. While Bunny and Poke guarded the villagers the rest of the team went systematically through the occupied dwellings searching for ordnance and food supplies, in the end finding nothing extraordinary. The people watched nervously, chattering among themselves, the women clutching their children. The animals meanwhile resumed their normal behavior, some of the ducks even approaching and looking up at the intruders with tilted heads.

Injun had entered the huts too, but took no part in the searches. They were standing inside the last hut. Injun said to the LT, "Sir, these people are so uptight they're about to shit their pants. They stink of fear. I doubt if there's VC in the area, but everybody's still camped inside the perimeter like they're scared of being outside or they're guarding something hid in here. Food or weapons. I can't tell. It's a funky scene."

As Injun and Hillbilly watched, the LT poked a pile of clothing with the barrel of his rifle. He looked inside some boxes that contained only the usual candles, matches, kitchen utensils, and other odds and ends. He scraped the outside edge of his boot across the dirt floor making a deep furrow he thought might reveal a hidden trapdoor to a pit containing a cache of weapons or food, perhaps even a tunnel. The soil was spread evenly and had been swept recently. Nothing.

They left the hut and all gathered outside its entrance. "Okay," the LT said. "Let's everybody hit that last hut, Bunny and Poke too. Looks like storage, so be thorough."

As they approached it a middle-aged woman emerged from the door waving her arms and screaming in a high pitch, "*Les cochons! Les cochons!*"

After weeks of hearing the harsh clipped speech of the Vietnamese, this brief burst sounded euphonious. "That don't seem like gook talk," Hillbilly said.

The LT put the butt of his rifle on the ground, while continuing to grip the barrel and looked at the woman. "It's French," he said. "She's calling us pigs. She probably learned some French in a Catholic school and doesn't know how to call us pigs in English. She knows we're Americans, and no doubt she'd like to."

As they stood conversing in the harsh sunlight, she ducked inside the door and emerged brandishing a sickle. Now screaming in Vietnamese, she ran directly at them.

Death is a shadow that taps you once on the shoulder. Without hesitating Hillbilly raised his rifle belt-high and loosed a single round into her chest. She died instantly, her words having had no more effect on her fate than the air expelled in saying them. The report, lifted and passed along on the molecular shoulders of the humid air, reverberated a long moment.

The LT held the event with his eyes until it stopped quivering, then enveloped and drew close what now was already a memory. "Goddammit, Hillbilly, you didn't need to do that."

"But she was attacking you, sir."

"With a fucking sickle. Any of us could have disarmed her, for chrissakes. This is no good. Do you hear me, *no good*!

"I'm really sorry, sir," Hillbilly said. "I'm really fucking sorry. I never killed nobody before." He sat in the dirt and started to weep.

The LT squatted beside the woman. Remarkably, she was still standing, propped against the wall of the hut like embodied grace, one leg straight and holding her erect, the foot aimed straight ahead, the other bent with the foot pointed away at a right angle as if ready to rise into a pirouette. Subcutaneous tissue at the bullet's entry site had been pushed outside the wound. This and blood droplets that had traveled in a reverse path of the bullet's trajectory showed her position having been close enough for blowback to occur. The LT rubbed his eyes. Her hair ruffled suddenly like the feathers of a gull turning backward against the wind, and she looked like something recently risen on the back of a sea creature ennobled in its wet flapping mange. Huddled in that thin shirt she was waiflike, a strangely persistent parable about suffering and transience as if nothing had comfort or value. Without turning around, he said, "Poke, call in for evac."

They left her there and entered the hut, poking absently at objects with their rifle barrels. No one spoke or made eye contact. Hillbilly belatedly joined them, still sniffling and wiping snot on his sleeve. His face was red and lumpy from the heat and the chronic acne that had made it a pockmarked moonscape from which even the bacteria sought escape. Feeling a confused, undirected anger the men began overturning boxes of kitchen utensils and hand tools and smashing ceramic pottery with their rifle butts.

Underneath some wooden crates stacked on the floor they found a trapdoor. Injun, who was standing idly by, came alert. "Don't touch that!" he yelled, but too late. Poke was already raising it when the world erupted. There was a deafening sound like a giant strumming railroad tracks and a searing light of penetrating whiteness. It was as if they had stepped into an ontological x-ray from which all pretentious flesh had melted away leaving just an essence. What is a human body? A sack of guts and organic juices, lair of a mythical soul. The prelude to death hurtles toward you with a furious roar, but at its denouement death itself whispers. We lean forward to hear: a cajoling, an abrupt cessation of time, and finally a black emptiness stretching to infinity.

How will we recognize the Apocalypse? What if it looks like an ordinary day, one with only the usual terror? What if it knocks and we aren't home?

Only a very delicate person can enter the empty room where there is an empty mirror, and with such lightness, with such absence of self, that his image leaves no mark.

Clarice Lispector, *Água Viva*

PART TWO

The Denouement

I live alone in a tiny shack a weak-armed stone's throw from the train tracks. The air inside is manstale. I don't remember how long I've lived here, but a while. My house has no mirrors. Had there been a mirror it would surely recoil at my image, which exists in another dimension beyond reflection. My beard—if I could have grown one—would have been black when I arrived; now it might be white. I'd give anything to grow a beard, do anything to hide my face.

I was born and raised in this miserable coal camp, or so they tell me. I don't recall a childhood, and my life story comes with a caveat: I'm the most unreliable of narrators, not that I could ever speak or think in such terms. Don't interpret what I say literally—the specific words and phrases I use. If you did you'd be reading a lie. I'm not thinking them, so don't assume they emanate from logical patterns of thought. I'm not capable of that and maybe never was. What and how I think is irrelevant. Thoughts can't be heard, and no one is listening to what I say aloud because I don't say anything; I can't.

At the VA Hospital over in Logan the doctors tell me I was brain-damaged in the explosion and likely won't recover all my marbles. Do I care? Not particularly. My future was always doubtful, but so is everyone's. What would I have done? Gone into the mines like the rest, probably. And considering my present appearance I'd be grateful for total anonymity, which seems impossible even here, a bleak valley doubtfully even God could find underneath the smog from the slate dump. Occasionally a drunken miner off shift tells a mostly incoherent story that includes the early me. He tells it from a bar stool in the Smokehouse Grill. I assume these reminiscences are true even if their retelling seems mostly autobiographical and I'm presented as a passive bystander. Apparently the childhood I don't remember wasn't memorable.

Can memories be forgotten? If so, were they ever memories? All he could recall clearly since his return were certain nights at the Smokehouse Grill. The war was a kaleidoscope of flashbacks interspersed with emptiness. They alternated in patternless scenes as if a plow had cut deeply across his frontal cortex leaving the broken synapses to reassemble randomly, pause for a time, and reassemble again in a different configuration. But which events? And when, exactly? What could they mean? Had he imagined even his memories?

The months of recovery in the burn unit of a U. S. military hospital in Germany were also a blur. He lay prone inside an oxygen tent, forearms perforated by tubes delivering nutrients and drugs. Morphine ameliorated some of the pain, although at times it was hard to know. Days and nights blended seamlessly as if time had stopped, which it does on arriving at the edge of a Black Hole in space. His visual memory retained an image of that blinding white flash that seared his flesh and induced pain so intense as to border on the exquisite.

Pain defies description. Had anyone in humanity's long history experienced such pain as his? Impossible. How could it be? His pain was a manifestation of Earth's ancient beginning; there can be no pain comparable, nothing so magisterial, so pure and profound. His auditory memory retained a thunderous boom that had caused his eardrums to rupture and his brain to resonate violently inside his skull. The disturbance generated a pressure wave that lifted his body and sent it hurling through a fragile bamboo wall of the hut. The disturbance penetrated his tissues to the cells of his very essence, setting into discordant resonance the molecules comprising every bit of his physical being. But odor is the most primal sense, and his most vivid sensations were the smells of cordite and hydrocarbons ignited during the fierce internal compression of that IED, and the stink of himself combusting.

In the few lucid moments of those early weeks in intensive care he believed he might be dead, except for that persistent pain so intense no descriptors were possible. Perhaps he had indeed arrived in Hell. Each pain-sensing nerve seemed exposed and unprotected. The light touch of a clean sheet draped carefully over him by a nurse or orderly, even a puff of air when the door opened and closed, activated them and set off a pattern of excruciating agony. He tried willing himself to rise off the mattress and fly to a place where nothing could touch him, but not even angels can fly on one wing.

Who was he, and what was happening to him? The medical staff came and went silently in the half-light, turning him over at regular intervals and shifting the positions of his limbs to promote even healing, daubing and moistening the embryonic skin slowly taking hold. They seemed inured to his screams provoked by these gentle ministrations. He wondered if the dead are merely paralyzed, lying in places like this fully conscious and able to hear everything, feeling acute pain but unable to speak or scream as if shot by curare-tipped arrows. Why couldn't they hear him? He found later that his screams had been imaginary, his larynx and vocal cords having been scorched past ever functioning. His only utterances had been soft moans devoid of any discernible emotion. His expression, once a bottomless reservoir of affection, was now fixed like an insect's. There can be no ambiguity, no facial signifying. Following these sessions the intensity subsided, sinking slowly as a flat rock in still water, wobbling, its edges lifting briefly in relief before tipping downward and pressing once again on every insatiable nerve. This was life imitating art imitating death.

His outer ears had been burned away, but the

middle and inner ears remained functional except for an extreme and persistent tinnitus that never went away. Voices and other sounds would always seem muffled and distant, as if emanating in a distant room. He learned later that listening to music helped assuage the effect, in part by overriding and damping some of the ringing's audio frequency and intensity, and by a shifting in focus temporarily outside himself.

Combat training in combination with the hearing disability had induced a heightened startle response. This and his increasingly strange and disturbing dreams were symptoms consistent with post-traumatic stress disorder. After PTSD had been added to the roster of his maladies the medical staff took precautions to alert him overtly of their arrivals and departures so as not to frighten him and risk rupturing the new skin grafts.

One morning, when he had recovered his faculties, an attending military physician entered his room carrying a thick file. The doctor drew the curtain of the oxygen tent aside, pulled a chair close to the bed, and sat down. "I thought you'd like to know what happened," he said. "Nod for yes, shake your head for no." He nodded.

The doctor opened the file on his lap and began recounting events of that day. "There are always holes in how stories are told and recorded afterward. Field personnel are under considerable stress, as you can well appreciate. Stuff sometimes gets muddled, people remember critical moments differently, and so forth, but what happened to your fireteam seems straight-forward—to a point. Then things get hazy. Maybe when you feel up to it you can add your own report to the file and reinforce what we have already.

"Anyhow it appears one of your men shot and killed a civilian female. Which man, and why did he do it? We don't know. Your mission was to search the ville for weapons and food cached by the VC. In doing so you guys entered a hut near where the woman's remains were later found.

"Someone apparently located and opened a trap-door to a cache pit. The door was booby-trapped with two M61 grenades and one Model 308-1 napalm grenade, all our own ordnance, of course. Where the gooks got it, who knows. The cache pit had been dug with an undercut, meaning it was roughly circular with an overhanging edge all around. Try to picture a tire lying flat; in other words, hollow in the center.

"The grenades had been placed beneath the over-hang. When they exploded most of the shrapnel went into the ground, but the napalm erupted directly upward. Base commanders knew this after later secur-ing the area and investigating the scene. In addition to collateral fatalities they found four dead Marines and you, the only surviving member of the fireteam. Shrap-nel wounds were less severe than might be expected. Yours were minor. If it weren't for the burns you'd have been down maybe a month at most. Bottom line: whoever set the trap could have done it better.

"Your RO had called in evac, evidently right

before the explosion, telling base to use the ville's coordinates, that there wasn't time to establish and secure a landing zone but the scene appeared to be clear. Dustoff got there within thirty minutes, assessed the situation from the air, and dropped into the unsecured LZ beside the blast. Except the crew came in hot. Charlie, concealed in a half-acre of elephant grass, did his best to turn a steel chopper into Swiss cheese. The dustoff crew was on the ground less than three minutes, just time enough to shove all of you—or what remained of you—through the door and then haul ass without additional casualties. Air support came in right behind them and fried the place.

"Some body parts were left behind and never recovered. Arms and legs had been blown into the lower branches of a tree hanging above the hut; heads had been separated from corpses. Not unusual under the circumstances. During the mayhem on the ground there obviously wasn't time to collect everything for sorting out later, and only one body, a big black dude's, arrived whole at base and with dog tags. Alongside you and the other crispy critters, even his original skin color was in doubt at first. The rest of the tags? Blown to hell, I guess, including your own. Adding to the confusion is your blood type, which is common and same as the other four guys on the team the Marines have yet to ID for certain, you included. We know who was there, in other words, but we aren't exactly sure who is who for tagging and shipping back to the States. Three bodies were similar in height and weight, so far as could be determined. You're apparently taller and slightly heavier although still slender. Guess a fat bush Marine is a rare animal.

"The in-flight corpsman asked the co-pilot to radio ahead requesting first-line medical standing by, that your condition was past his pay grade. He'd managed to clamp an artery or two, establish an IV of fluids and antibiotics, and shove a couple of syrettes of morphine into you. He also staunched bleeding here and there from mostly superficial frag wounds with wads of gauze, but he was in over his head.

"Medical personnel stabilized you as best they could. Luckily there was an emergency load of crispies being lifted out of Saigon for Germany in a few hours, bound for our special burn unit here in Hamburg. A spot was reserved for you at the last minute. That's why you aren't in the States. It's how triage works sometimes. You're one lucky bastard to be alive. You'll be here several more months for grafts and recovery. There's scarcely any unburned skin on you left to use. The burn unit is doing all we can, but crispies are never easy, especially when they arrive extra well-done like you. To tell the truth, you shouldn't have survived. All odds were against it."

The doctor stood. "Back to identity confirmation for a second, then I'll leave you alone. Your uni-forms gave no clues to rank because you guys were practically naked. Nearly every scrap of clothing had either burned away like tissue paper or fused to your skin. Not enough left to determine rank. Maybe you know who you are, but the Marines sure as hell don't. We've concluded tentatively you're Private First Class Danny Boy Beaver. Indicate yes or no by moving your head because we'd like to clear this up."

Why did his thoughts never end in conclusions but hung instead in perpetual suspension? Inside me, he thought, is a switch that shuts off prematurely, a light that dims while I still need to see, a bell that doesn't ring when I push the button. Not even the possibility I still might die arouses me. They say if I become infected by any common hospital bug I'm likely a goner. Am I really a lucky bastard to be alive or simply a corpse in waiting? In my situation is there a difference? He knew this for certain: had he died in 'Nam his one request would have been, leave me to decompose and fall as rain, not whither on a desiccated trail under a vaulted blue sky in the dry season. My scorched skin screams to leave this cot and float just above the soft sediment of a cold mountain stream while the water flows over, around, and under me.

What a callous prick the doctor was. Did he think graphic descriptions of his comrades in death would not affect him? We don't get used to death, he'd wanted to tell this asshole. Not ever. He couldn't say for certain whether Danny Boy Beaver was or wasn't his name. It seemed familiar, but he couldn't remember. There was so much to remember. When he didn't move his head the doctor shrugged and left, too important to leave behind a comforting word, too busy to wait for his tears.

Ben Webster

In a dream he found himself in a small park beside the sea. Other than some gulls the only presence was a black man sitting alone on a bench and wearing a rumpled brown suit and brown derby hat. A black object beside him could have been a miniature coffin, but his eyes were watering from the healing facial wounds, and he couldn't tell. As he came closer he recognized it as a musical instrument case. Around the man's neck hung a strap attached to a tenor saxophone. He was fingering the horn but not playing it, watching his fingers depress the keys as if composing something in his head, something still too premature to be born.

A thick mist spread across the cobblestones and planters of dwarf Alberta spruces kept short by genetics or by God and forced into sharp secund relief by the wind. The man heard his footsteps and glanced up, startled at what he saw, on his face the puzzled look of a bleak and ragged saint exiled suddenly from solitude.

In dreams he can speak. Shocked at his own audacity he said to the man, "If you play that thing to nobody and you're deaf yourself, there's no sound."

"What?"

"Can't be any music if nobody hears it. A smart man once said so."

"This man of yours, he wasn't damn so smart. The gulls, they hear it."

"Yeah, but to them it's just noise, not music."

"God hears it."

"God got ears, huh?"

"Hell yeah, just because your own is burned off don't mean you wasn't made in His image. And He hears all the prayers. You don't do that without ears."

"Didn't know He heard prayers. Sumbitch never listened to mine. You talk to God, huh?"

"Not me. I'm too scared, but ain't God's voice that terrifies me, it's his awful hollow silence. And I ain't foolish enough to hold out false hope of redemption, thinking I might already be standing under a holy light and suddenly see His hand reach down and hear Him say, 'Come on up, old son.'" He shifted his weight on the bench. "What might be your name, nightmare? Mine's Ben Webster."

"Danny Boy."

"Like Daniel in the Old Testament? I see something else wrote on your jacket."

"No, just Danny. They don't put the frontal names on your clothes."

"And Boy, what's that, a nickname?"

"Middle name."

"Well, Danny Boy, there's two things you don't

need to tell me. One, you're a cracker. And two, I know your last name."

"How's that?"

"The first from your cracker accent. The second because your last name is stitched right there on your jacket, dumbass."

"They tell us they do that so we don't forget."

"I can well believe it. Okay, ain't none of my business, Danny Boy, but how did you come to get named that?"

"My mama's favorite song." He thought he recalled a scratchy record playing endlessly, the arm of the record player set so it repeated endlessly. He still remembered the label that read, *Master Desmond Casey, The Phenomenal Australian Boy Soprano.* Either that or somebody told it to him. It could have been either, but doubtfully both.

"You calling me a nigger, Danny-my-Boy, it's hurtful."

He didn't remember doing that. There were many holes in his dreams. "I didn't mean to hurt."

"Well, it sure as hell come out that way."

"I don't see how because I didn't say it."

"Then that's the difference. I say you did. Seems simple now, don't it?

"I reckon."

"You reckon."

"Who do you play your tunes for, Ben Webster?"

"I play mostly for me, but sometimes for love, or a half-assed recollection of it. Love never happens like you want, never like it ought to. Love always turns out gritty, man. She telling you to take a bath or shave or get your goddamn stocking feet off the coffee table. Don't leave no empty beer cans laying around, she tells you. And her? You hunting after a sweet smiling woman wouldn't say that shit, get me? Better to write about love than ever live it. Even better to blow it through a horn. I once seen love looking at me from a open door, and I was too scared to stop walking. When I finally turned around she wasn't there. So I crawled up into the light where the world looked the same except brighter. Don't ask what I mean because I couldn't tell you."

"I know what you mean, and you got everything wrong." He told Ben Webster that if she'd been the woman he loved he'd have gone through that door and licked her all over until there wasn't a dry place left on her, and when he reached the end of the last toe he'd start over to be sure he hadn't missed a spot, guaran–damn–teed. He'd lick her until his saliva held her immobile as a twig in a nest stuck together with swallow spit. His candor startled them both.

"Well," Ben Webster said slowly, "there's a drop of hope in you, cracker. You done stopped seeing life in monochrome. My woman was a beauty, but she was black from the top of her head to that very last toe. Now all you need is to find a pair of lips and a tongue that works proper. Otherwise you can't neither lick somebody nor play the trumpet, 'cause baby, this chick run off with my trumpet player."

He felt mute, impotent, because just underneath his skin was something related to Ben Webster's music. A poor cousin, maybe, but something, and like a drowning swimmer it refused to surface. He was that swimmer, and in another dream he believed he had eventually surfaced and crawled home caked in unatoned guilt and river mud. Why had he alone survived?

Ben Webster said, "The average human face has a proper nose, but yours seems reduced to a matched pair of breathing holes. Makes it easier to clear the snot out, I guess. And the rest? I hear tell they can cure acne with vitamins. You might of tried them before getting your entire motherfucking face burned off. That was a little extreme, don't you think?"

"Now it's you being hurtful. Feel better?"

"No, I ache some, and anyhow I never said it." So said Ben Webster. He unclipped the horn from its neck strap and set it aside. He stood and waved his arms up and down vigorously, took several turns around the bench, and sat back down. Ben Webster was a portly man but his step was light, his feet seeming to tread a thin conveyor of sliding air.

A yellow claw of moonlight bent down. The sea lapped at the land like a stray dog licking a wound. It stank of rot and centuries of European wars, of anamnesis where the poppies blow, bowed and bloody row on row, fouling the earth to overflow. . .where soldiers left their crumbling bones, marked now by rows of flattened stones. "I wish you'd die and go away," Ben Webster said aloud, or maybe he thought it, but he didn't seem to be speaking at anyone in particular. Could be the words were meant for himself or he wished simply for the dream to end.

He said to Ben Webster, "Where's your band? Why do you sit here by yourself playing a saxophone?"

"I did have a band once. But the bean-counters and cost-cutters and the gov'ment, they come along one day and pared us down to a single cymbal and a fourth of a pair of castanets. Now there's just me and what I call my bandstand, this here park bench. And my audience? That be you, baby. I can tell you're a joyful man. With that smile I bet you gets all the gals."

He remembered a movie in which strange birds—birds from some little-known place in the world—danced in courtship. Background music choreographed their movements, little dance steps and hops, the synchronous entwining of their necks together to squawk something only another bird could understand. "There's really no fucking music," he said, and gestured toward the out there.

"It's always playing, baby, you just got no ears to listen."

He licked the mouthpiece of the sax as a hound licks a bone all over before settling down to gnaw. "What's the matter, cracker, you just got a funny look. Don't like being around NEE-groes?" It was true, in the coal camps all along the bottom the coloreds lived in separate hollows, never as neighbors.

"Don't try to shit me, Ben Webster. I only have one

look, and it never changes. I like them fine, I guess."

"You guess. Would you trade places with me?"

"I ain't thought much about it, but I might. Take a close look. Being me is worse than being a Negro, for sure."

"Hey, cracker. How'd you like if I called you a nigger? Wouldn't matter. It ain't the same because I'll always be what I am, but you a white man, a *caw-ca-shun*."

"You looked at my face lately, *nigger*? Bring on Jesus and his miracles. I'll trade with you any-time." Without his being aware, night had entered his dream. A tree branch peeled back in the wind revealing a sliver of moon. Then he remembered, he remembered it had been night. This was the second moon he had seen, or maybe the same moon twice.

Ben Webster's lips worked at his reed like a goat nibbling a carrot. "I confess I ain't looked at you close. It's too hard on the eyes, sorry to say. You ain't a pretty sight even in the dark. Switch places, huh? Be warned, it hardly pays to be dark-skinned in a blinding landscape where only ghosts and the pale living are visible. Look around and tell me if you see any other NEE-groes excepting myself. Even the fucking gulls is white. By the way, cracker, you know that sound when you hold a seashell to your ear? They tell you it's the sound of the sea, which is bullshit. It ain't the sea, it's the echoes of your dreams.

"God give you a set number of breaths, hear me cracker? It's a set number, and He don't tell you how many that is. I'd rather use up mine blowing this horn, know what I'm saying? And you? You done wasted a whole bunch telling me I'm a nigger, which ain't exactly news." He blew a riff, a minor celestial revelation in e-flat, then decoupled his lips and let the sax slide to one side. "And that's about it, baby shakes, life from my side of the tracks. I ain't hardly beside myself with joy or the Lord's word or anything else, but I'm at least a musician, and you ain't jack-shit."

He held up a hand. "Now hold still. I ain't finished. A man's memories come on fast and hard, slip-sliding through the fog, disappearing and suddenly coming into focus but always looking different. When you live hard and feel hard you use up life and die quick. The heartbeats of a hummingbird versus those of a tortoise, you heard that story. The Lord only passes out so many heartbeats, same as he does breaths, and if you ain't careful you'll use them all up young, sooner rather than later. Or if you just don't care you can use them up all at once on a woman or a war.

"Life be a song, baby, and you too deaf to hear it. It be the music of the words that matters, not the story. In fact, jazz don't tell a story in a conventional sense. Ever notice that every rock and roll tune sets out a little story? Well, jazz is different. A jazz tune is endless, its message never reaching pause. And the story's always the same, give or take. We're born, we sing, we die. Between the bookends of birth and death, what can vary except the melody?"

His anger and hurt dissipated the instant Ben

Webster closed his eyes and blew another riff. "What's the name of that?" he asked.

"'Soul Time' is what I call it, but I don't know its real name. Nobody does. There's a piano and a bass you probably can't hear, but I hear them clear and clean. Can a person hear smoke? I don't know that either. It's like names. You tell me yours and it won't matter. You can walk away with your name and I wouldn't miss it one damn bit, but I'll miss the notes on the air you leave behind. Soggy ones today. Yeah, today I gotta hunt for my tunes in the fog." He put the mouthpiece to his lips and blew some more. Fog and measured hesitation trailed behind the notes, syncopated to the motion of a slow-stepping cat.

"What do you think about, pumping out tunes?"

Ben Webster let his horn fall slack and brushed crumbs off his jacket. "Mostly pussy and the sharp taste of sour mash. If one don't cause you grief the other will, and their order ain't important, first or second. There's no thirds."

"My eyes are blurry. Where did all the color go?"

"Sonny, there's only color in music. Everything else is black and white, same as you and me. Anything in between they call dreamtime. You think it's there but it ain't. Just the Sandman piping in your head. At night we all alike. Your eyes can't see colors in the dark. When you hear the wind off the ocean, that's me. So listen, listen up for 'Cotton Tail,' baby, then you know you alive. A man walks beside his own rhythm and manages to keep up if he's lucky. I'll play this last tune and then I'm leaving."

"Where will you go, Ben Webster?"

"Far away," he said before closing his eyes again and starting to blow.

The Reeperbahn

He first knew of Ben Webster through what might be defined as a waking dream, a state when the mind teeters between wakefulness and sleep. He liked waking in darkness, rising and gaining buoyancy until breaking through the surface into consciousness. On this night a record was playing at the nurses' station down the hall. His door had been blocked open to allow a change of air, and the music was unexpected. He was feeling better. The burns were slowly healing, annealed by encroaching patches of new epidermis and scar tissue that would eventually build a barrier between the outside environment and his raging nerves.

When the duty nurse came to check on him he motioned at the door and pointed to where one of his ears had been. The nurse was a young black man. He said, "The sounds?" Seeing a confirming nod, he said, "That's my man Ben Webster on tenor sax blowing breathy and soft, one way you can tell it's him. That's Art Tatum behind him on piano. Tatum died back in, I think, fifty-six. 'All The Things You

Are' is the name of the tune. Mr. Webster blows what jazz buffs call a 'tasty' horn. It means about what you'd think: rich and organic with a delicate finish, like vintage wine. I wanted to study music but switched to nursing. More job opportunities and steadier pay. Even in the military it's a decent gig. Man I don't go anywhere without my sounds. Is it too loud?"

He shook his head as vigorously as he dared. The orderly laughed and showed him a thumbs-up.

Another few weeks passed. Autumn had arrived, going on a year since "the event," as he thought of it. The pain was attenuating, and the staff had begun weaning him off opioids. He couldn't speak and could eat only soft and liquid foods, but that would change once the scar tissue around his mouth had formed and stretched a bit and his throat had healed completely. After he could get out of bed and move around he was put on a program of stretching exercises to prevent the scar tissue on his torso and limbs from stiffening and eventually restricting movement. He performed these regularly under direction of a physical therapist. His feet had been badly burned, resulting in ampu-tation of all his toes or gangrene would have surely taken them. He had lost all but the thumb and index finger of his left hand; on his right all that remained were the three central fingers. In practical terms he'd been left with an incomplete set of mostly immobile claws, the nails of which had turned thick, striated, and brown. He was able to hold a cigarette, although lighting one was still difficult. He considered quitting smoking, then thought again. What the hell, he told himself. Everything is going to be a major chore, why not this too?

With his nostrils burned away his sense of smell was at best rudimentary. Still, he occasionally caught a whiff of vomit from the hall, strangely frightening, a reminder that life is lived from the inside out, that a smile can be illusory but puke is real. And for some unexplainable reason he could smell the sea, perhaps an accessory experience beyond landlocked olfaction.

He had a primitive urge to feel warmth, the buried seed's urge to shove its green shoot into sunlight. On warm days he shuffled outside where he and other recovering burn victims sat on benches in a pleasant patio. Their new skin was tender, and the attending nurses made certain they were adequately protected from the sun. Without the prospect of participating in a conversation he sat alone avoiding the others who had formed friendships, which was fine: he felt no need of social interaction. One of the staff had found a Marine boonie hat in the lost-and-found, and he wore it to shield his face.

A van took those sufficiently mobile into the city twice weekly and later picked them up at a designated location. The passengers comprised a dozen or so barely ambulatory monsters, permanent social outliers anywhere except in a circus. Hobbling in walkers, leaning on canes, swinging on crutches, they formed a brotherhood that found a common identity in grief and barely masked self-pity expressed in blustery sarcasm. The van had been christened the "rolling freak show," and its occupants challenged each other to see who could draw the most horrified stares once loosed among Hamburg's unwary pedestrians. Theirs was a fraternity from which each member who departed eventually for the indifferent World was replaced by a new recruit arriving from the incendiary jungles of Vietnam. Each new victim brought a story he assumed was unique, only to discover later had been told countless times.

He accompanied his comrades just once to collect his ration of stares from the Germans. The van dropped them at a location along the Reeperbahn, a mile-long tourist-driven freak show of its own that cuts through the center of St. Pauli. There among the honky-tonks and brothels they drank beer for three hours, or in his case, tried to. Holding the glass took both hands. Attempting to sip from it through remnants of lips was still more difficult, but he did manage to pour some of the beer through his partly exposed teeth; the rest escaped down his neck.

After that experience he declined subsequent excursions, although the Reeperbahn had left an impression. His dreams became so increasingly sensate and rich in details that he often awoke wondering if the events were entirely imaginary. But that was impossible. In his dreams he walked normally and at a normal pace instead of slowly shuffling on ruined feet. And he could speak and carry on conversations, although whose voice emanated from his mouth was never certain. It seemed a composite of several, but if so, which component was actually his? To confirm his wakeful state he punctured the silence with little chuffing sounds.

Often his dreams seemed to be someone else's, as if his own life had been strangely juxtaposed or merged with another man's, and he wondered dimly if during "the event" his soul had miraculously grabbed another's and held tightly as it rose, freed suddenly by death, his own a hanger-on in half-death. More disquieting, he realized dimly that dreams require perspective and are the engines of stories, but he had no stories. They had been erased.

The Reeperbahn he dreamed was not the one he experienced. His imagination had invaded and changed it. He knew the street was located on the River Elbe and that Hamburg, one of Europe's major seaports, was sixty miles inland from the North Sea, but it seemed a coastal city in his dreams. Not only had the river disappeared, so had the jostle of intrusive humanity and its machines. The Reeperbahn he dreamed was also a far less populated place.

From this new vantage point he stood along the edge of the street looking down at the sea. To the immediate right was a single flight of stairs to the beach. He took them, emerging onto damp sand. The tide had receded, and behind him was the seawall covered in drying rockweed. Someone had hung a soldier's medals by pushing pins through their ribbons into crevices between the stones. Spray-painted in large black letters above them was a single word in English: WHY? The North Sea, its surface unbroken and undulating like a metallic gray blanket, was reflected in the sky; on the horizon a dull cloud bank hung suspended in tawdry stillness.

He came to a section of beach thick with seabirds and stepped into them. They rose in a flutter of white confetti as if he was seeing them at a distance. The exposed rockweed emitted an odor of salt, iodine, and decay. Could he have read about this somewhere? Not likely. Any memory of the senses requires immediate reinforcement and can't be a dream or a story told by a stranger. Therefore it must be a true fragment of his own imagination and not another's.

He continued walking, noting the base of the seawall where the last high tide had arranged the decaying rockweed in a pattern of persistent death. He came eventually to another set of stairs near a long stone jetty perpendicular to the beach. The stairs led upward and back onto the Reeperbahn, where under a Hefeweizen sign depicting a prancing unicorn he fell to the pavement and puked up his guts. When he looked up a thick fog had erased the line separating sea and sky, and from his prone position all he could see were thigh-high shiny boots, facsimiles of Hitler's guilt now forgiven. In this confused state he thought of kissing them.

Now horses circled at full gallop in sunlight. He bought cheap notebooks, but finding himself illiterate, abandoned them in subways and beside newsstands and parking meters. He knelt abjectly on sidewalks listening to the rain and waiting for something to happen. Back on the Reeperbahn a whore approached, face a troweled mask, the calf of one black stocking punched through revealing white fat, her teeth a tannic swamp. She asked if he wanted a blowjob. When he didn't reply she dropped to her knees and like a sow began rooting in his trousers, unearthing instead of truffles two wan testicles. She kissed him afterward with lips like compliant strips of warm liver. On them were the remnants of his own spurts, on his own an aftertaste of jackboots.

A thunderclap accompanied by a recurrence of that exploding white light in his brain suddenly woke him. Shaking with fear and not yet fully awake he imagined his detached arms and legs spinning upward as if in flight, lingering momentarily in the branches among those of his comrades. Oh, if I could fly to them and join their frayed edges to my own ragged surfaces. If I could just once call out to you in my hoarse voice of a shattered bird.

The Revenant

In spring he was discharged with a permanent disability pension, compliments of the U. S. military. Thank you for your service, a hospital administrator told him. *Semper Fi!* When you get home, clock in at the nearest VA hospital to get your name on the roster and arrange for regular checkups and to keep your scrips current. All the necessary paperwork, including your military records, are in this envelope. Don't fuck up and lose it. In fact, sleep with it; don't let it out of your possession even to take a shit. There's an Air Force transport leaving Hamburg for the States tomorrow. We'll take you to the airfield in the van. Be ready to saddle up at oh–seven–hundred. Once in the U. S. you'll connect with a Marine transport to Camp Lejeune. I believe you're familiar with the place. You can rest a couple of days at the base hospital (paperwork's in the envelope), pick up some new clothes and accessories, and muster out. Someone there can arrange to get you on a Grey Dog to West Virginia. It's been a pleasure. Good luck.

That evening after chow he made the rounds

making gestures of goodbye to the staff and his fellow inmates. He was now on his own. The next morning he left; everything went as planned.

The bus let him off at the one-lane bridge over the creek. He shouldered his single small duffle and walked across its thirty-foot length and into the coal camp of Scalded Creek. Directly ahead was the company store. It was around noon, and several miners off shift sat on the steps drinking beer and smoking or chewing tobacco. Their conversation stopped as he approached. He ignored their stares and entered the store. An older woman stood beside the cash register leafing through a movie magazine. She looked up at him, startled, and replaced the magazine in the rack. He produced a folded sheet of paper, handed it to the woman, and nodded for her to open it. On it was printed, I AM DANNY BOY BEAVER. WHERE DO I LIVE? He pointed to his mouth and shook his head, indicating he was unable to speak.

The woman held up an index finger and said to wait there. She told him she would get the manager. He could hear their low conversation from a back room. She was evidently preparing her boss for what he was about to encounter. They emerged together after a minute, the manager smiling. "Welcome back, Danny Boy," he said, holding out a tentative hand then quickly pulling it back. "Uh, I knowed your folks. They're in the cemetery over yonder. I believe you can find the way if you're here thinking to visit them. Of course, because they've passed on to their rewards another family moved into your old house. You probably ain't heard of them. They come from somewhere around Boone County."

He had been prepared for this, and pulled from his shirt pocket another paper on which had been printed, I WANT TO BUY A PLACE OF MY OWN. Most of the houses were company property and rented by the miners and their families, but a few were privately owned. The rental of company houses was restricted to employees. The manager nodded and handed back the paper. The company store manager at Scalded Creek served functions other than his store duties. He was notary public, real estate broker, de facto mayor, rent collector, and general go-between for those needing to connect with a lawyer or insurance man. This last service he performed gratis considering everyone in the camp was a captive store customer and tenant and indebted through him to the company, not to mention being a friend or relative.

He leaned on the counter and lit a cigarette. "There's a shack down the train tracks just before the tipple. It's in pretty good repair. There's three rooms, well water, and a outhouse in back. Of course it's noisy as hell around there. The tipple's running three shifts now with the war on, and the trains come by so close you could reach out and shake hands with the engineers, if you was so inclined. But you know about all this. Folks, they get used to it. The place comes with the small piece of ground it sets on. Not much. You might grow some termaters and such in the summertime. As you know, our water is sulfur water and ain't fit to drink, so you'll need to tote jugs from the spring like the rest of us. At least you won't have far to walk. I reckon you're on disability and won't be going in the mines, but you can maybe work on this place and fix it up some."

He held out his hands to show they were useless. "I see, well I could find a miner off shift to do what repairs you think is necessary, for a small price, of course. What do you say? Want to see it?" He nodded. "Well sir, let's go. Myrna, watch the store, will you?"

He picked up his duffle, but the man took it from him gently and slung it over his own shoulder. "Let me. It's the least I can do for a war vet. Guess you had a right tough time over there. The place is just down the tracks. If you're up to it we can walk." He nodded agreement. "By the way," the man said, "My name is Grady Snodgrass. I been here near all my life and knowed your folks, Remo and Glossie, and you too before you went in the service, but I guess you don't remember me."

He held a finger to his temple and made a circle.

"Okay, I get it. Them war injuries can do you a lot of damage, mess up a man's body and mind both, but no matter. You'll get your memory back once you're living here again. And I'm sure the folks will help out as they can. We're all good Christian people here in Scalded Crick."

The shack was old and unpainted, its boards warped and weathered a dull gray, but its lines were straight and the walls and superstructure sturdy. The inside was unfinished and not insulated, and daylight leaked through spaces between the boards. The place had been vacant for years, and everything was blanketed with coal dust blown in from the tipple and passing trains. Particles of coal dust crunched like sand under their shoes.

The sitting room had two double-hung windows, the other two rooms one each. In all of them generations of spiders had usurped the corners. The rooms were small, but adequate. The main door off a porch opened directly to the sitting room. In the center was a coal stove set on firebricks and vented through a ceiling block. Beside it was a battered ash bucket and small shovel. Off to one side stood an old table covered in peeling linoleum. There was an empty bedroom with a closet. The kitchen was equipped with an ancient gas stove and a sink with a counter, most of which was taken up by a hand pump connected to the well. Through the kitchen door at the back of the house and down a short path was the outhouse.

He made a dollar sign in the air, opened what was left of his hands palms up, and shrugged. The price? He had saved most of his money, nearly thirty-five hundred dollars, and was assured of a disability check the rest of his life, easily sufficient to live on.

They were standing in the sitting room. Grady

lit a cigarette and exhaled smoke at the ceiling. "The owner is Miz McCourtney. She must be close to ninety and lives over to Mason. This place belonged to her papa, and she's been looking to get rid of it for years, but there ain't been any buyers. I told her honest, who'd want to live in a shack practically setting on the train tracks and not more than a hundred yards from a tipple? I'd say in this case it's a buyer's market. She's been wanting twelve hundred dollars, but she inherited the place so it don't owe her nothing and vice versa. Whatever she gets for it is gravy, far as I'm concerned. And she sure as hell ain't kept it up. I'd say offer her a thousand dollars. And because you're a vet and unable to work I won't take any commission."

With his single index finger he wrote $800 CASH in the dust on the table. Grady nodded. "Seems fair. Hang on a minute." He went into the kitchen and worked the pump handle. Rusty water squirted into the sink. "The pump works, but I'd yank the handle a bit to flush out the line if you was to buy the place. No telling what's crawled down in the well and died. Meanwhile I'll try to find you a place to sleep. Anyhow you won't be drinking the water. What's that you're saying? You'll stay here? I don't reckon there's any harm. I noticed a broom in the closet. Maybe you can sweep out a corner to sleep in. I'll get your offer over to Miz McCourtney soon's I can. Coming back to the store? You'll need some goods and a jug to carry water."

He arranged for Grady to keep his money in the store's safe. It was wrapped tightly in a bundle in such a way he would know if the piece of newspaper covering it had been unwrapped. No point in letting anyone see how much was there. He bought some food and a few other items, nothing too heavy, and stopped to fill the jug from the spring, which was near the tracks and on his way. Locating it was easy: people of all ages were lined up where clear water poured continuously through a pipe from a spring inside the mountain, falling a couple of feet into a shallow makeshift basin of loose stones. On seeing him they stared shamelessly, and some of the children laughed behind their hands, stealing glances then looking away, knowing they were being rude but unable to resist. That response, he figured, would eventually be replaced by ordinarily looks and eventually hillbilly lassitude. When that time arrived his wish to become invisible would be fulfilled; he will have blended into the landscape.

He needed to spend a little time in the shack to get a sense of the surroundings. The tipple, lit up like an aircraft carrier, crashed, rumbled, and bucked through every hour of the day and night as it crushed the newly mined coal fed into it by conveyors at the mouth of the mine. It separated and discarded the accompanying slate while retaining the coal, which was sieved to lumps of proper size and washed. Sometimes this job of separating the slate was performed manually by "breaker boys," kids who had quit school and gone to work at the mines. The finished product, shiny and black, was loaded onto another conveyor and dumped into waiting railway cars. Trains pulling out from the tipple creaked and groaned under their loads as they passed the shack, blowing their whistles to warn anyone walking the tracks to move off. It was like living at the center of a massive beast whose intake, digestion, and excretion never stopped.

Grady had pointed out a singular advantage of this location. "At least it ain't beside the slate dump," he said. "You'll still smell the damn thing, and it's still close enough for the smog off'n it to burn your eyes when the wind's on you, but at least it won't be directly in your backyard. Thank the Lord for small blessings, huh?"

Slate, which is associated with coal seams, is a waste product of no value and simply hauled away from the tipple and dumped at a convenient location. Slate is incombustible, but because some coal always remains even after separation, slate dumps inevitably catch fire, usually from spontaneous combustion, and once burning they never stop. As more slate is added to the pile, so is more fuel. Even abandoned slate dumps often smolder for years, filling the air with gray smog that turns sepia under sunlight.

Legend holds that Scalded Creek and the eponymous cluster of hardscrabble shacks along its banks were named when hot embers at the leading edge of the slate dump, having inched into the water like a relentless lava flow, sent up a permanent plume of steam visible from far up the mountainsides on all but the windiest days. When one morning during fall butchering season a long-forgotten miner stepped out of his shack and said to a neighbor, "I bet a feller could scald a hog in that crick," the name stuck, or so they say.

Owner

He swept a space on the floor and opened a can of baked beans, chewing the contents slowly. Eating and drinking were still difficult and always would be. He was getting accustomed to what his fellow victims in the burn unit called "life in the slow lane." Although still a young man he would never again run, jump, even walk without risk of stumbling. But at least he could get around without mechanical aid. At least he hadn't ended up in a chair.

Still, the absence of toes renders balance precarious. At Lejeune the new gear he requisitioned had included a pair of tennis shoes, a therapist at the hospital there having recommended them as the most effective footwear for someone without toes. They would require adjustment in his gait. His military-issue boots were stiffer and added a measure of support, but now he needed shoes that were lighter and more amenable to stepping along railroad ties. Following the train tracks by walking along between them was the most efficient means of navigating a coal camp, and he knew he would never own or even drive a car again. Walking between the tracks was his only option.

Night fell, but the tipple, a small city within itself, dominated the camp. He felt he could adjust to the constant noise, but the intrusive light was another matter. He would need shutters or window shades. He had just fallen asleep when the floor started quaking and a blinding white light pierced the bedroom window. There was a deafening shriek that seemed to penetrate his skull and start his brain resonating. He let out a muffled scream that seared his throat and curled into a ball hoping to become invisible. With a pounding heart he awaited the incoming missile, the approaching angel of death that would explode on impact and vaporize his flesh. Ah, you idled slowly in my dark spaces, carburetor a marvel of everything serene and sleek, and now you've come for me. Then it was gone. The room darkened; the quaking of the building and ground underneath it subsided. Thunder that had seemed to cascade across an endless acoustic plane dispersed into the distance. A coal train had passed by.

He lay on his back smoking, head propped on his duffle, listening to the tipple imbibe, chew, and regurgitate. He heard the railway cars shake and rattle as coal poured into them, heard them clang and clank as the line was pulled forward and empty ones dragged into position underneath the conveyor. Just before dawn another train passed. Despite being prepared for the impending chaos he could feel his heart again nearly abandoned his chest. Even awake and forewarned he was unable to completely repress those primal fears hammered deep into his subconscious by the war. Would they ever dissolve into his liminal psyche and fade away? The more immediate dilemma was whether he could adjust to living in a place where the triggering stimuli assailed him relentlessly and with such fierce urgency at all hours. If the nightmares extended through waking he was lost. Somehow he must learn to adapt and function.

Even during quiet times the same nightmare came repeatedly. In this dream the monster was silent, formless, nothing but a void. It never spoke or made threatening gestures, but became terrifying by its seeming absence, and he awoke straining to scream.

He spent the day in the cabin pacing in his new shoes and listening restlessly to the tipple, trying to calm himself when the trains passed, his despair a patterned wretchedness repeated like the squares of a quilt, always in front and opening in sequence, never ending. Except they had to end. There was no choice. Wherever he went there would be these explosions of white light in his brain that in turn ignited autonomic sensors into expressions of unbearable fright. Every clap of thunder would bring an instant upwelling of terror and anticipation of dismemberment and death. How many times could he visualize the limbs of his comrades—now joined by his own—hanging in that tree and not go insane?

Around suppertime he started walking down the tracks, thinking he might stop in at the company store. Maybe just seeing Grady and Myrna would ease the suffering. But the store was closed, so he continued on, stepping aside for a coal train while trying not to look at the terrible grinding wheels and imagining them as engines of destruction. A little way past the store stood a rickety structure leaning over the creek. A worn hand-painted sign hanging from the top edge of the porch identified it as the Smokehouse Grill. He left the tracks and took a path down from the railroad bed to the door.

The place was dark and dingy, as if illumination had been long forbidden. Natural light had once been a possibility because there were several windows, but they were covered in such thick films of black dust that they might as well have been boarded over. A bald overweight man stood behind the bar drying beer glasses. He was whistling absently through his lower teeth, a soft sound without form or cadence, perhaps the love song of an ancient swamp creature spilling out its discordant sorrows.

On hearing the door close he glanced up with a startled look. The glass fell from his hand and shattered on the floor. He stared a second at this new presence. "Well shit," he said, and bent down with a labored grunt to sweep up the broken pieces with a whisk broom and dustpan. When he stood he was again composed. Smiling, he said, "You're Danny Boy. Grady told me you was home when I was up to the store today. Welcome back. I can see your time in gook country warn't easy. Let me buy you a beer. Grady says your memory ain't right just yet, so in case you forgot, I'm Owner." He drew a dime draft and set it on the bar. "The regulars will be in directly, I reckon. Never knowed them to miss a evening's arguing and haggling and acting unchristian towards one another. You'd think none of them had any friends. It's peculiar, but I reckon you're familiar with this bunch. Your daddy was one of them until him and Glossie passed away, bless their souls. So you have my sympathy twice, once for losing your folks both at the same time, and for the goddamn war you got mixed up in. But all that's history now, except for your wounds, of course. I guess the gov'ment give you a disability. I hope so. It's the least they could of did, give a man with your wounds a disability."

Owner said, "I think I'll just join you," and drew himself a glass and leaned on the bar, towel in hand. "You was just a boy when you went off to the Marines, I recollect you coming in here to say goodbye to your daddy the day you left for boot camp. I seed you standing for the bus out on the hard road. Seems like a lifetime ago, don't it?"

He nodded agreement, then he made eating motions.

"You hungry? Grady done told me you can't talk and dropped some memory besides. Must've had your throat scorched in whatever fire burned you up. Must've of hurt like all hell." He reached under the counter and produced a menu.

He looked at the items and pointed to the burger platter.

"You like your burger with fries or slaw?"

He shook his head.

"Fries then?" He nodded.

Owner shouted through a service window to the kitchen, "Burger platter with fries, Burris."

So this was the start of his next life. Each of us occupies an empty room all his own where the intake of our breath and our exhalations are counted and recorded until their allotments are used up and suddenly canceled. So Ben Webster had said. Where our laughs, screams, and sighs are monitored by the silent walls. Each wears his room like an invisible shroud; it trails us everywhere, moving with us in lockstep. Our rooms encompass the microorganisms living on our skin and in our bowels. Despite all this they remain empty because we ourselves—what we consider to be consciousness—are never in occupancy. It's the eternal paradox: we seem to be here, but in truth no one is ever home.

Those other beings, what are they? Phantoms like ourselves, dreams passing, no more substantial than clouds; noises arriving fleetingly, then gone, the moment itself gone forever, never to be repeated.

Thaddeus

He concentrated on the mechanics of sipping beer while Owner returned to dishwashing duty. The simple act of drinking was still anathema. No matter the angle of the glass, a good portion of its content spilled down his neck each time it was tilted. He caught Owner's eye and made a motion of wiping his mouth. Owner understood at once and came to his rescue with a small stack of paper napkins. He had tried using straws in Germany, but soon gave that up: without proper lips to form a seal there was no way of generating suction.

His meal came, and although it was finger food to other people he motioned to Owner for a knife and fork. He could only masticate tiny bites and began laboriously carving up the burger and fries after applying liberal amounts of salt, pepper, and ketchup. Consuming it would take a good hour.

He heard a commotion behind him and turned on his stool. In the open doorway a large overweight man was attempting to jostle a much smaller man in a wheelchair into the room, but the front wheels had turned sideways and stuck. The man pushing the chair backed it off and made another attempt. His imprisoned passenger was clearly agitated. "Goddammit, Thrice, how many times have you done this?" His companion, grunting more from his efforts, gave the chair a final successful shove into the room and wheeled it to the bar. "I see you, Danny Boy, and I'll say a proper hello when this fat moron and I get rightly seated and are holding alcohol. I'm Thaddeus, as you already know, and this shithead who can't steer a simple wheelchair is Thrice Twice, my faithful idiot companion. Okay, Thrice, now let's find out if you can maneuver me over near my personal stool without fucking up. Christ, you might as well be a hairball coughed up by New Jersey."

The open door let in a whiff of slate dump air, which smelled surprisingly fresh, along with a measure of coal dust aerosol. The interior of the Smokehouse had that odor of enclosed spaces occupied too long by errant humanity and tempered by sin-beckoning smells of whiskey, cigarette smoke, unemptied ashtrays, soiled bar rags, old cooking grease, and wooden flooring caulked tight by decades of tobacco juice and spilled beer. The edge of the bar had been whittled by jackknives until ragged as a hillbilly's bite.

Those who bellied up had choices of a dozen tattered stools bolted to the floor, torn seats crisscrossed by duct tape. Directly in the middle separating them into two groups of six was a vintage barber's chair. From it Thaddeus, a man given to prolixity, imbibed and held forth as if enthroned. Thrice had rescued the apparatus from a junkyard and tinkered with the hydraulic mechanism until the chair moved smoothly up and down. During a moment of rare tenderness and generosity Owner had permitted its installation. In its lowest position the seat was the same height as Thaddeus' wheelchair, allowing him to scoot onto it and once positioned pump the handle and raise himself to bar height.

Thaddeus did just that, then with minor effort shifted his torso and reached down to pull in and arrange his sticklike legs. Thrice sat down on the adjacent stool and sighed deeply. Owner brought draft beers for the three of them.

Thaddeus was agonizingly thin and shrunken and wore the look of a distracted but noble count newly lost in the woods. His complexion had that pale sickly color seen on cadavers and shut-ins. "Well," he said, "so you're home, if anyone could consider this god-forsaken shithole a home. Cheers." He tipped his glass and took a swallow. "Every busybody in Scalded Creek knows your story: war veteran, horribly burned and disfigured, looking to buy Miz McCourtney's old place down the tracks and offering to pay cash, planning to live on military disability and become a nuisance to the community by making us pity you. I have to say that as the only cripple in Scalded Creek I don't intend to share my allotment of grief generously."

Thrice leaned forward and turned his way, the better to see him around Thaddeus. He said, "Have the busybodies done missed anything? Any gossip we ain't been told about?" He showed a gap-toothed grin: "You wouldn't be hiding out from the law and that's just a disguise, is it?"

He shook his head with sincerity and raised his glass to Thaddeus and Thrice, reminded of the sarcastic ripostes tossed around in the burn unit. The counselors had told them how injections of humor could help rebuild self-confidence and hasten psychological recovery. Confidence, they had been told, is nothing more than a feeling that a decision you're about to make is the right one.

Owner, who had been monitoring this opening conversation, looked at him and shook his head. "Better get used to it," he said.

Feeling dizzy after another beer, he decided to return to the shack and rose to pay the tab, but Owner held up his hand. "Not tonight," he said. "This is on me. I figure you'll be back and I'll have other chances to take your money."

He felt good. He now had three friends, four including the unmet new friend waiting on the porch, and the buzz was helping too. When he stepped outside a brown dog hobbled over wagging its tail. It was an exact replica of the pariah dogs of Vietnam: brown, short-haired with a curly tail, lean, and feral-looking. He bent down and gave it a clumsy pat on the head. The dog licked his hand. He stood in the open door, pointed to the dog, and raised a hand palm up.

Owner said, "Oh, he's a stray. Been around a couple of weeks. Scrawny, ain't he? Reckon he ain't been eating regular."

He closed the door and started up the path to the train tracks. The dog's right hind leg was deformed and couldn't touch the ground, but he hobbled alongside on the remaining three, both of them stepping slowly and methodically. When they reached the shack he let the dog inside, fed him a can of beans, and gave him some water from the pump. That night they slept curled together on the floor, and when the first night train came rumbling and shrieking down the tracks and he awoke in terror the dog nuzzled his neck in a seeming gesture of comfort. Right then he decided to keep the dog but not name him. What would be the point if it could never be spoken? A name has no intrinsic meaning. Someday, if he ever became certain of his own, he might reconsider.

Chester

A few days later when he stopped by the store Grady told him that Miz McCourtney had accepted his offer. All they needed now was to drive into Mason to pay her lawyer and sign the title. Grady said he'd drive him there and back and do the notary work for free. By afternoon he was standing in front of the store in possession of the only property he'd ever owned. The dog was waiting on the steps and appeared to read his expressionless face.

The company store stocked nearly everything anyone needed, and Grady could order what it didn't have. He bought the necessities in only an hour or so: a bed with pillows and two sets of bed clothes, a ten-gallon container with a spigot at the bottom to store spring water, lamps and light bulbs, lamp tables, a kitchen table with two chairs, kitchen utensils, a toaster, coffee pot, fry pan, pot with a lid, two five-gallon buckets to carry coal, and a coal bucket to store coal beside the stove. He also bought a refrigerator. Because Grady promised to deliver everything he stocked up on canned goods. The only luxury items he bought were an easy chair with a footstool and a record player.

Autumn was coming. Grady got the electricity turned on and arranged for help fixing up the shack to prepare it for winter. An electrician at the mine agreed to rewire the house when off shift, charging a flat fifty dollars plus materials. An off-shift carpenter and all-around handyman insulated the walls, put up drywall, and afterward painted the interior The man repaired, repainted, and rehung the windows so they opened and closed smoothly and replaced the glass of two that were cracked. He also installed black shades that blocked the lights from the tipple and trains on that side of the shack. He replaced some worn shingles and made sure the block where the stove pipe penetrated the roof was secure and still fireproof, and arranged to have a pair of propane tanks delivered to fuel the kitchen stove. Finally he ripped up the old linoleum throughout and laid down new material. When the work was finished the place was brighter than it had ever been, although beating back the coal dust that crept in all around would be an endless task.

These two men, by now his friends, had offered to install a water heater. He hesitated at first, then agreed. The hand pump, sink, and counter were taken out and replaced by a new sink with hot and cold fixtures and a new countertop. To avoid longer pipe extensions, the heater was put in a corner of the kitchen and hot and cold water lines inserted through the outside wall facing the outhouse and opposite the train tracks. There the men put in a metal stall shower that drained directly into the yard.

By the time cool weather arrived he and the dog were enjoying all the comforts and had established a routine of sorts. He lacked only a washer and dryer. Those were installed a month later outside the other kitchen wall, set off the ground on concrete blocks topped with plywood and protected by a lean-to shed, the back wall of which was the house.

They awoke early. After a trip to the outhouse and showering he made coffee and fixed two scrambled eggs with fried ham and toast. He had breakfast at the table in the sitting room while the dog ate canned food in the kitchen. Depending on inclination more than needs, they either walked the tracks collecting coal spilled from the trains or they went to the store. The post office was also in the store. Grady cashed his disability checks, put the money in the store's safe, and withdrew the appropriate amount each time after he shopped. Grady once told him that he was the store's only customer who paid cash instead of buying on credit and having it deducted from his paycheck. On the way home he and the dog invariably stopped at the spring. With those damaged hands he could only carry a single gallon jug of water at a time.

His miner friends had returned at his request and built a small coal bin beside the washer and dryer, also in the form of a lean-to, where he accumulated coal so that in the coldest weather he wouldn't need to collect it. If there was any advantage of living beside the train tracks, this was it. Spilled coal was always there for the taking, and it didn't require walking very far. The trains passed on schedule, so the spills were replenished regularly. There would always be enough to warm his shack no matter the outside temperature.

The days turned consistently overcast as winter settled in and the hollow was without color, almost without light. The limp steam lifting off the creek was instantly ripped to fragments by the wind. The smog from the slate dump seemed to possess a mass appropriate to its leaden hue, requiring all his strength merely to stand and push his arms and legs forward through its pressing density. He bought a winter jacket, more undershirts, a pair of jeans, and a couple of hooded sweatshirts, and on his head was the boonie hat he'd worn all through recovery in Germany. He couldn't imagine ever parting with it. On the coat rack at home it had a hook of its own.

He had long since discovered that most questions directed at him could be answered without needing to speak, and his interlocutors soon got in the habit of posing them so that his yes and no replies, or questions he posed in return, were complete, needing no qualification. Everyone picked this up quickly, turning what might have been awkward attempts at dialogue into smooth monologues from their end, requiring him to answer simply in nods and shakes of the head and with gestures.

Nearly every evening he went to the Smokehouse for a simple supper at the bar, usually a burger with fries. The dog came too and lay quietly on the floor underneath his stool. Owner didn't mind, remarking more than once that the dog was better behaved than some of the customers. Occasionally he even rewarded the dog with remains of a burger left uneaten on someone's plate. One night he said, "The dog got a name?" Unwilling to reveal his secret, he had shaken his head. "Well, he's a damn good dog," said Owner, "and I'm proud to have him a regular here at the Smokehouse Grill." Then looking pointedly at Thaddeus and Thrice, he added, "Maybe this here dog could learn y'all some decent manners."

Sometimes their group was joined by Chester, a black man who lived up Nigger Holler, which intersected and lay perpendicular to the hollow containing Scalded Creek. It too was owned by the mining company, but the men worked side by side without strife or animosity and everyone bought on credit at the company store. All the children attended the same school. It was only the housing that was segregated. Chester, he learned, often drove the trains that rattled his nightmares. Chester suffered from vitiligo, which had made most of his face an unpigmented white mask. Probably because of this they had formed a warm if unspoken friendship based on mutual sorrow and affliction.

The trains now had a human face, and although resembling a mask it had two ordinary human eyes that emitted no blinding light, and a quiet voice quite unlike the coal trains. He would concentrate on remembering this as he fell asleep. Maybe their frightening thunder might attenuate to indistinct mumblings as heard through a distant wall, their blinding cyclopsian eyes dim until they cast only harmless shadows. Broken memories of that day in the ville haunted him especially on very still nights as he paled into unconsciousness preparing to become the ghost we all become in dreams. When asleep he ceased to exist. And then the trains came, and he was startled awake in the middle of that nightmare.

Twyla Ray

One night at the Smokehouse Thaddeus turned to him and said, "Was Twyla Ray a girlfriend of yours? Then neither of you quit the other? No? Then I presume we can talk bad about her and say what we think and think what we say. Am I right? I take from that shrug it's okay." He shook a little salt into his beer to make it bubble and foam some at the edges.

Thrice broke in and leaned around Thaddeus: "It's just that once somebody seed the two of y'all holding hands. That was right before you went in the service."

He nodded.

"Well," Thrice continued, "You wrote her some letters from over there in Vietnam, and she brung them in when her and Randi Sue was both waitressing here and passed them around. It was nice of you to say hidey to us all. Right nice. And we appreciate that, don't we, Thaddeus.

Thaddeus said, "We do indeed. As my learned friend here says, it's always pleasant to be included in someone's thoughts, especially from the other side of the world. You wrote her several letters as I recall.

Did she ever write back? No? Well that doesn't surprise me because you'd hardly stepped off the bus in Parris Island before she ran off and married Weasel. I doubt you recall Weasel. He used to work cat-eye shift driving a shuttlecar. Then he quit mining and later folks said the two of them moved down to Jolo where he got a job selling used cars. Didn't like the mines, I guess, but I bet he liked the good money and steady paycheck, and I bet Twyla Ray liked it even more because after a time she was back living with her folks. Selling cars puts a man on straight commission, and you know what that means: no sales, no paycheck."

Thrice said, "Before they left I hear tell she once blowed Weasel in his overalls after he come off shift and surfaced with a coal-dust moustache. And unbeknownst to her she wore it plain as anything when she went shopping up to the company store. I believe it was Grady told me. That must've been some sight." He slapped his hand on the bar and barked out a laugh. "My cousin says she's spent so much time laying back on the seats of pickups that she can tell you the make and model by the ceiling upholstery. I used to look at her regular when I'd come in here, face all acne and built like a railroad tie. No tits where a man might take comfort, but Lordy I'd give my left one to find out what the fuss over her is all about."

Thaddeus said, "Rumor has it you lost your left one in Korea in fifty-two and been flying unbalanced ever since. Anyhow with those leg muscles she'd have clamped you tighter than a roof bolt. You'd probably exsanguinate through your earholes."

Owner, who had been eavesdropping, now butted in. "Could be Weasel and Twyla Ray never went to Jolo a'tall. Remember how he liked to read and such? Kind of weird in that way like Thaddeus? A old boy up to Davis who said he's Weasel's uncle, I believe, was in here a while back and told me Weasel went off to the university up to Morgantown where's he's studying on oxidation and homosexual poets. Seems like he'd make more money selling cars."

"Whatever the case," Thrice said, "we need to get to the bottom of it and find out what really become of Twyla Ray during that time, if only to quieten the rumors."

Thaddeus said, "All I know is a couple of years back or maybe a little more, just after Danny Boy left us to partake of jungle life, she disappeared and didn't come back for several months. That's before we heard about Weasel and her supposedly having a thing, if you get my meaning. Rumor at the time had her knocked up, but nobody could put a finger on who the daddy might be because she wasn't seeing anyone, at least openly. Some of us figured it might be you." He turned and looked at Danny Boy, who shook his head. He couldn't recall even coming close to having sex with her, although she was surely in his fantasies during the time in Vietnam. She must have been. "Well, anyhow she eventually came home the same circumference as when she left and without a kid squalling in her arms, but we'll likely never know the reason for her absence, unless it really was Weasel."

Thrice said, "It's just strange, that's all, a young woman up and taking off without telling nobody where she's went, not even her family. Her folks was worried to death and after a few months they give up on her, figuring she was dead somewheres in a field or beside a road. Owner, I'd like a burger plate, if you please."

"But you just ate one," Owner said.

"I know, but all this talk has me desperate for another."

He and Twyla Ray had encountered each other once in the company store. She got that horrified look strangers do on first seeing him, but her reaction had been unusually severe. Instead of resuming her nonchalant examination of the grocery shelves she had abandoned her cart and backed away toward the door, hands covering her face and staring wide-eyed at him through splayed fingers pressed against her face. Apparently she wasn't living with Weasel, unless he was in Scalded Creek again, which according to local wisdom he wasn't. In fact, no one knew where he was or much cared.

Conversation at the Smokehouse that night moved on, as it usually did when one subject had been discussed, argued, or insulted into exhaustion. He discovered that if he showed up regularly one patron or another—or sometimes several at once—occasionally revealed bits of his history. The details were usually contested, considering the unreliability of the narrators, but it was at least something, and given time these scattered fragments could eventually form a crude mosaic of his life before the war.

If he arrived late the place might be filled to capacity, especially on weekends when families occasionally enjoyed a rare night eating out, the regulars squatting as usual atop their barstools like pithed amphibians while the jukebox blared country tunes and dirty-faced children chased each other among the tables. Coal was king, and anyone who wanted a job could get one. Life, you could say, was bituminous.

Owner

The name on my birth certificate says I'm Phil B. Slaughter. Shouldn't be any surprise that my family and friends called me "Philby" growing up. I own the Smokehouse Grill. Have since fifty-three when the Army let me out with a honorable discharge. I'd been assigned to a NCO club over in Korea where I learned about running a bar. You know, ordering supplies, checking stock and maintaining inventory, pouring drinks, keeping a ledger, matching cash took in against receipts at the end of the night, and trying to keep order amongst a pretty unruly bunch of young soldiers on the loose from home, a lot of them for the first time.

Now folks just call me Owner. That loudmouth Thaddeus named me. I was always yelling at the fellers about one thing and another, such as not to spit tobacco juice on the floor but use the spittoons setting around for that purpose, and not to whittle the bar top. Sure as shit when I told some smartass to stop this sort of stuff he'd say, "Who says?" And I'd say, "I say, and I'm the owner." So at first they called me Owner Phil just to get my goat a little, and finally just Owner, even them that's knowed me as Philby practically our whole goddamn life together.

Some claim their time in the service was wasted, but not me. I learned a lot, and when they mustered me out I come straight home to Scalded Creek and bought the Smokehouse from a couple of retired miners who thought that because they was experienced drinkers it qualified them to operate a bar. They extended credit to their deadbeat buddies, didn't pay no attention to inventory, and added on a couple years of personal experience as drinkers before going bust. That's about when I got home and bought the place on the cheap.

I'd saved some money while in the service. Hell, a man had to be stupid not to. The food and bed and clothes was free. You got medical care, and with my job I could drink all the beer I wanted without paying a cent just by holding a glass under the tap. Being in the Army didn't cost me nothing but a couple of years I'd have truly wasted going in the mines if I'd stayed home and went 4-F. And considering I never saw action over there, being a soldier was a lot safer than crawling inside a mountain and digging coal where the goddamn roof can fall on you any minute of the day or night. Yessir, I done alright during my time in the service, and I'm still doing right good. I got no complaints. I know all about running a bar and restaurant, and the first rule of business I obey like it's the Eleventh Commandment is NO CREDIT. See that sign on the wall behind me? That says it plain as the nose on your face. There's friendship and there's business, and I keep them separate.

I know my customers work hard. Coal mining ain't no picnic, but that's none of my concern. Folks sometimes ast for a little credit until their next paycheck, and I always turn them down. Why, if my own mama was to ask for a short beer on the cuff, know what I'd say? I'd tell her, "Sorry, Mama, but we ain't knowed one another long enough." That's a joke, of course, but when I tell that to the person asting me they get the idea pretty quick.

Money's always tight for my friends and neighbors, and I understand that. I do the best I can to keep prices reasonable and maintain a clean family atmosphere. I ain't out to make myself rich, just earn a decent profit that matches the effort I put in. I aim only to follow the Lord's mandate, meaning to prosper and multiply my kind. Still, you can't keep people from gossiping and bitching about one thing and another. Disagreements is part of human nature, I reckon. Even Jesus had his differences with the Pharisees, who got down on him because he wouldn't wash his hands before supper. And another time Jesus lost his temper and drove some money lenders out of the Temple. I reckon at some point everybody, even the Son of God, gets fed up listening to bullshit.

I won't try to piss up your leg and say my job is all hunky-dory. The bar business has its troubles too, its crosses to bear, a Christian person could say.

The help nearly always steals from you: food, cash, liquor. Whatever can be slipped into a back pocket, stuffed in a handbag, loaded in the trunk of a car, or swallered on the job. The only honest employee I got is my cook Bullis, who lives up Nigger Holler and is here seven days a week from eleven ayem till closing. He ain't never missed a day since I hired him maybe six, seven years back, nor stole from me, that I know of. I suppose Randi Sue is honest, and probably Twyla Ray was too when she worked here, but they was always fighting between theirself over tips, one accusing the other of not sharing.

And sometimes the customers ain't exactly pleasant. My heaviest crosses is probably Thaddeus and Thrice, my most loyal patrons. The two of them show up every night, rain or shine, snow or sleet, dependable as the mailman. Neither was ever married, and I got to say that somewhere around there's two damn lucky women. They own their own houses but got nowhere to eat a proper supper, so this place is it. And they got nobody at home to fight and argue with, so they come here to scrap with one another and whoever else they can drag into their disagreements, including me.

Thaddeus just don't give a shit about what comes out of his mouth. His aims was always false anyways, trapped up there in his cabin atop that washboard road halfway on the mountain. Living in that chair day in day out, sucked dry with polio looking at a bare incandescent light bulb dangling out of the dark of the porch, probably looking to him like a lonesome firefly trapped behind glass. I reckon you can't blame him for not caring. It ain't much of a life, nor Thrice's neither.

They're a odd pair. Thrice used to be a rigger in the mines till he got too slow and fat to climb around on the equipment, so he opened him a mechanic's shop down the tracks alongside the crick where he fixes stuff, cars and pickups mostly, but he'll fix anything that runs on gas or diesel from a lawn mower to a busted-down bulldozer. Just don't tell him you're in a hurry because then he'll sure as shit put your job on the back burner. Thrice don't like taking orders nor being hurried.

Want to hear something funny? Well, funny in a odd way. Thrice had a identical twin brother whose name was Onely, as in the number one. He was the first born. If you're curious about how Onely and Thrice got named, the story goes like this: Nefferson Twice was standing beside the granny woman helping his wife at the birthing and looked at his newborn son. In a instant of drunken wonder and without hesitating, he said, "That's Onely." And when a second son popped into the light unexpected not five minutes later he blinked and said, "And that's Thrice" because it had sounded, well, biblical, or so the granny woman told everybody. I reckon Nefferson understood that giving the second kid the first name of Twice would of seemed like a pointless doubling down. Imagine being named Twice Twice. Now Triplets might of been a different story.

Onely died a great overfat lump on the seat of a
bass boat over to Bluestone Lake maybe two year ago,
victim of a sprung heart. His fishing buddy claimed he
toppled backwards and expired after seeing a mermaid
surface, fingers and toes lavished with petals of pink
water lilies. Her eyes, Onely is said to have described
with his last breath, had no whites to them. They was
set far back in the skull all glittery and strange like
chunks of coal. Who can say what actually croaked
him? Maybe it was the sight of bare titties and pond-
weed hair that stopped his ticker cold in mid-thump.

But Thaddeus, he's my heaviest load, heavier than
Thrice and weighs half as much in actual life. Most of
what he says is probably horseshit, and what's left is
guaranteed to be. Poor bastard's been crippled with
polio near all his life, although he's likely to tell you
different given a chance, as if history lets a man invent
other choices and ignore what really happened. Him
and Thrice, they're near the same age and the three
boys, including Onely, growed up together tighter'n
peas in a pod. Then Onely and his old woman moved
away after he retired from the mines, and only Thrice
and Thaddeus was left to torment me.

Thaddeus and Thrice live side by in houses halfway up the mountain they bought off the company.
That was during a time when the mines was cutting
back. Thaddeus don't drive, of course, so Thrice carries him everywhere he needs to go. Grady's helpers
at the store deliver his groceries so he don't need to
shop, and he gets around inside his house just fine in

that wheelchair. Thrice even rigged a device in his van that hoists Thaddeus inside it while still setting in his chair and bitching at full throat so he can carry both their worthless asses down here to the Smokehouse and put pain in my life.

Thaddeus has some education, two years of junior college over to Logan where he studied on accounting. If ever I have a problem with my books he lends a free hand, but not without a whole lot of hollering and complaining about the inconvenience and how busy he is. He worked keeping books in the company's branch office here in Scalded Creek and retired on a nice pension. Got lifetime medical care besides. He's set for long as he lives.

Thrice tells me Thaddeus' house is full of mail-order books and that he's always reading on some odd subject or another, mostly stuff the average person wouldn't understand or pay a nickel to know about. He's a smart man, I give him that, and if you didn't know better you'd think he wasn't from around these parts but come from a big city full of educated people. Sometimes after he gets a few too many drinks inside him—which is every night—he turns all full of hisself and becomes downright obnoxious, insulting folks left and right. It's a wonder somebody ain't bopped him out of pure exasperation, crippled or not.

Then recently Danny Boy come on the scene. Grady says he just showed up to the store one day from the hard road fresh off'n a Grey Dog with a sign he pulled from a pocket saying who he is. He could tell a terrible story sure as hell if he could talk, but a war explosion over in Vietnam fried his voice box. He won't be joining the choir anytime soon. Danny Boy's in bad shape all around, cooked to a cinder, and don't really remember his life here amongst us.

And we don't remember him very good neither. He was Remo Beaver's boy. Remo was a mean sumbitch, snarling at other customers and at Danny and sometimes smacking Danny's mama around. Her name was Glossie Beaver, and her and Remo got killed when their car went over the edge and crashed in a holler. Happened when Danny Boy warn't more than a few weeks in the Marines.

His folks was about the same age as me and Thaddeus and Thrice. In them times lots of kids got the earache, but not so much nowadays. I don't know why that is, unless most of them faked it to stay home, and one was Danny Boy. I remember Remo telling us here at the bar that he'd say to him, "Horseshit. Get on to school and listen to the teacher out of the ear that don't hurt. And quit whining or I'll bop that sore ear till it rings clear to Christmas." Yeah, he was a mean sumbitch alright.

Danny come across as a quiet boy back in the day when he used to sneak in here like a whipped dog and tell his daddy it was suppertime. If Remo don't smack him upside the head outright he always hollered at him to get on back home and tell his mama to keep supper warm, that he'd be there when he damn well felt like it. I guess the main thing I recollect about

Danny Boy is that despite his youth he carried on him a heavy burden of weariness.

Thaddeus

"I recollect him being a mite shorter. Yes, I do." Thrice was thoughtful, standing beside his stool instead of sitting on it. He leaned a forearm on the bar and with his free hand salted his beer. "This here first glass of the evening is bringing up a mental picture of him from them early days, clear and close, and I'm looking at it direct."

Thaddeus turned toward Thrice with a querulous expression. "Now just what the hell could you be yapping about?"

"Danny Boy, who'd you think?"

"Well, you might have said so. I'm not a mind-reader."

"I just said I recollect him being shorter than he is today. You got any opinion?"

Thaddeus said, "Of course I have, and my opinion says your opinion is wrong, as usual. According to my recollection he was taller before, and I'll tell you why. In case you haven't noticed he walks stooped over, probably because the scar tissue around his chest and stomach is pulling him over and down, or maybe his back was busted up. I'm told those artillery explosions can fling a man fifty feet or more. And of course he can't straighten his knees, which alone makes him shorter. War has a way of using up a man's stature and aging him before his time. Everyone comes out of a war bent and used, some more than others. Finally, he doesn't have a single hair on his body. It's all been burned away. He wears that Marine hat everywhere, but I've seen him take it off a couple of times, and he's completely bald, not even any scalp fuzz. Hell, not even eyebrows or eyelashes. A bald man is shorter because a goodly head of hair can add a couple of inches, at least."

"Maybe so," Thrice said. "I never thought of that. He does walk like he's stiff in the bones. I reckon he could grow a beard. A beard could help hide the terrible truth."

"A beard won't make him any taller, dumbass. Anyhow he can't. Those hair follicles on his face were killed along with the others. Guess that's one advantage: it eliminates the need to shave."

Thrice said, "In olden times they made a tea from burdock root or seed and drunk it to cure the clap. Must've been good stuff 'cause it was a fall blood purifier and healed rheumatism besides. And burdock was free. You just walked into the mountains and picked you some. Why, it growed in the pastures and even right along the roads. No doubt there's a plant out there that puts hair on a man's head slicker'n snot on a doorknob that modern medicine don't know about. Damn shame they ain't no medicines like burdock tea these days. Hell, today each disease has got its own special medicine and a special doctor to apply it, and ain't none of them is teas, only pills. And they cost money. We could still make them teas and tonics ourself, but nobody does anymore because there ain't no granny women around that knows how. They all died out, and hill people today, they can't tell one plant from another, except it's a corn plant or a termater. Betcha a old granny woman could mix up something and Danny Boy's hair would pop right back, a poultice maybe."

Thaddeus said, "As usual, you're full of shit as a Christmas turkey. If there was something out there scientists would know about it."

"Well, there's another way. Of course we don't know if Danny Boy's got any hair left on his ass, but seems to me them doctors could of grafted his ass onto his face," Thrice said. "Nobody would've much noticed the difference."

"Hear, hear! Now that's just unkind," said Thaddeus. "Did you say terrible things behind my back when my spine was crushed during that mine explosion in fifty-eight and I ended up in this chair?"

"Horseshit, Thaddeus. On that day you was sitting in a nice warm office in your wheelchair cooking the company books."

"Y'all shut your pie holes," Owner said. "He's coming in."

He entered, stamping off the mud and snow, the

dog beside him. The vacant stool beside Thaddeus awaited. The dog preceded him to it and lay down underneath. Owner set a glass of beer between his claws and placed his supper order by yelling to Bullis through the service window.

Thaddeus watched him settle awkwardly onto the stool and lent a hand pulling off his coat. "Ah, the apostate returns," he said.

Still only on his second beer, Thaddeus was already into it. "Many of you might not know, but I saw considerable action over in Korea. That's how I ended up crippled. Some believe it's from polio, but they're wrong.

"I'd been shot bad in the spine at Chosin Reservoir. The bullet exited by means of the navel, or nearly so. I now have two belly buttons where the average man can use only one. When MASH saw I was a useless cripple they exchanged me for a trained guard dog with a defective paw. Being paralyzed I can't do a thing about pussy except fall down before it and pray."

"I've heard it benefits them in your state," said Thrice. "Praying, I mean."

"Goddammit, Thrice, don't interrupt me. The best of us had attended Officer Candidate School, bolted securely to the swift discomfort of theoretical geometry and map reading. Cave painting and cuneiform scribbles in wet clay had been replaced by then with a system of Arabic symbols behind which hides real illiteracy. I remember how the professor's feet were set in a permanent splay similar to a clock's hands showing quarter-to-three, and he had this walk like something heavy was about to fall through his pockets.

"After graduation they split us up. I was assigned to a platoon led by a legendary officer with the bearing and patina of a bronze general on horseback. He walked with hesitant steps like the emissary of an insignificant nation, and to us students in our innocence he seemed scarcely alcoholic. No one knew his origin, but he was Southern in speech and manner, perhaps akin to a young Jeb Stuart, unaware of the difference between tragedy and farce so necessary to the grim North.

"Every morning at reveille he greeted us with ravenous goodwill. Turned out he was actually Texan with a nose pockmarked like those mounds of sand shaped by fire ants. Still, he was ungodly handsome with cruel blue eyes and a handlebar moustache turned early white from a tight sphincter and kept aloft in rejection of gravity by his own sturdy earwax. He collected the wax every night after supper using a tiny silver spoon and stored it in a rose-colored vial suspended on a chain among his dog tags. In the night a brave cigarette glowed in his mouth daring sniper fire.

"Our mission was to frag water buffaloes in the rice paddies, but you could only frag so many thinking they're hiding IEDs between their butt cheeks before the humans who own them get even more pissed than usual and take to shooting at you. Then there's the problem that maybe a buffalo has been force-fed some sort of incendiary device and is just standing there ass-deep in the water waiting for us to show up before lifting its hind leg to pull the pin and blowing everyone to hell.

"Suicide buffaloes were a major problem over there, and the survivors, they taught it to the monks in Vietnam, the ones who set themselves on fire. This water buffalo notion was all the colonel's. His nickname was Zany Zach, and our platoon leader was just following orders, or so he said. But I think he secretly enjoyed it. Each time we fragged a buffalo he gave a little shiver of hope, and his eyes retracted behind slits like a lizard's.

"We had left behind no remnants of self-pity, no ethereal regrets. Egos had long since been flushed away, leaving us naked and wrinkled as newborns. Sometimes the gooks ambushed us, but we were always prepared. We aimed true and shot them where they stood, and they fell dead among the duckweed and floating buffalo turds. We were on, I think, about our fourth water buffalo. Its horns were unusually wide, like Texas wide. About that moment I noticed one of the grunts muttering something and stumbling around in the ricey mud. He said his job was no different from gutting your average overfat honky during a drug buy except for the thick skin and the lice. He came from a frigid rust-belt city where the street lamps were always shot out and rodents were the dominant mammals. Although our politics differed, I admired his directness. True sincerity can withstand any rebuttal, even in the face of uncertainty and moral stagnation.

"I emphasize that the merging of zoology with ferreting out spy secrets runs in my family's blood. We seem to have a certain aptitude. My papa on mama's side was in the Army during the first Great War, a Cipher's Assistant Second Class. He told me they once intercepted a message about weapons of unimaginable destruction being shipped through the Rhine Valley by the krauts, and the colonel made them go out and shoot all the damn mules they could find and cut them open, but they never found any secret weapons, only mule guts.

"But back to my own tale. When they finally gave me leave I flew to Seoul. I was chair-bound, of course, but strong and handsome in my officer's uniform and laden with so many medals they nearly dragged down that side of my parade tunic. Women were all over me, then one in particular strutted past. I'd noticed her watching me lustfully from a distance, brushing off generals and admirals seeking her favors. She wore a dress resplendent in tits and legs. No one afterwards could remember its color, the room having turned monochromatic the moment our eyes met. I barely repressed the urge to throw her face-down on the dance floor directly before the orchestra conductor and chew through her hosiery, lick her vulva, sniff her ass, and drown in the sweet syrupy scent of reproductive hormones."

"You say she had big 'uns, huh?" said Thrice.

"Yep, a choice pair of *poitrines*," Thaddeus said, "which is French for women's breasts. Bet you didn't know that."

"Only because I don't need to know it. A man can only absorb so much useless knowledge."

Thrice was fidgeting to change the subject. "I hope to die abruptly and broke and with a hard-on," he said.

"You'll for damn sure die abruptly if you don't give me some elbow room," said Thaddeus. "I can hardly bend my arm. Come to think of it there's something gone from you. I can't press a finger against it but it's kindly and wretched and dear, like an old sweat sock saved from junior high school days or a rubber stuck against the wall behind the couch filled with your mummified homunculi. When I think of you I'm reminded how Earth has too many fucking people; on second thought, make that too many people fucking. Take your parents, for example. And now the scientists tell us our DNA still retains the buzz of insects, some more than most. So buzz away a little farther so this glass can reach my lips."

"Well, if you ain't thumping the goddamn bejesus out of it tonight," Thrice said.

"Mercy," said Thaddeus. "Two blasphemies in succession, a record even for you. I can tell you aren't a soldier of the Christ. In fact," he continued as if speaking from the top of a very tall tree or even Heaven, "the Lord God will read your evil thoughts, such as they can exist within the emptiness of your skull, and see that you fry in the eternal fires, real crispy like Danny Boy here. Son, you ain't got a snowball's chance. There's one hope: you might repent and renounce this impiety by getting down on your knobby knees and washing my feet."

"Jesus damn Christ if you ain't the all of it." Thrice shook his head and took a swallow of beer, sucking it loudly through holes where some of his teeth once resided. Their departure had given him an odd lisp, like sustained wind through leafless branches. "Why do you care about clean feet? You can't feel them anyhow."

Their food had arrived, and the conversation droned on. Thaddeus said, "Why would any sentient being put carrots in chicken noodle soup? Owner, come here! Would you please ask Bullis to remove these obnoxious orange roots from my soup?"

"Shut up," Owner said.

Thaddeus said, "There's an awkward dissonance about you, Owner, a false quiver of sincerity, leading some citizens of Scalded Creek to suspect you might vote Republican. But I'm prepared to let that gossip pass and chalk it up to ignorance." He turned to Thrice, who was dousing his French fries with vinegar. "What can vinegar on fries possibly achieve except to make your asshole acidic?"

"It's a start," said Thrice. "And if you don't quit pestering me I'll fix your chair so it won't roll. I'll put square wheels on it."

"Owner!" Thaddeus said. "I demand you expel

STEPHEN SPOTTE

the cretin beside me. In this age of enlightenment and cultural sensitivity he's belittling me for being a cripple. That's discrimination against the halt and the lame. Does he say disparaging things about others of us? You because you can't add and subtract? Chester here because he's a nigger? Danny Boy because he's a hopeless freak? Of course not. Far too clever for that, but cripples are fair game, defenseless in our immobility."

Owner continued rubbing the bar top with a grubby rag and saying nothing.

Thrice said, "I don't like you, Thaddeus, not because you're a worthless crip but because you're you."

"Owner, I take umbrage at that. Please tell him to shut the fuck up."

"I ain't neither of your daddies," Owner said. "Until one of you pukes on my floor, I don't care."

He admired Thaddeus' erudition, his confidence and bravado, but most of all he admired his handicap, his being a cripple with a normal face. People notice someone in a wheelchair, but they seldom stare. They might feel pity, but not revulsion. Did Thaddeus suspect how badly he wanted to exchange places, to hollow him out, climb inside his skin, peer out through his eyeholes, shout through his larynx? Thaddeus had sometimes looked at him as if observing from a place of secret knowledge, almost as if he knew something no one else did. Then he quickly reminded himself, who can ever remember exactly what he heard, saw, or said? He wondered how long he could continue this life with no apparent purpose. Then one evening Thaddeus offered clarification: "Your job here on Earth, and Scalded Creek in particular, is to simplify the agony of imagination by giving us something tangibly ugly to look at."

Thrice

We're setting at the bar of an evening. Danny Boy ain't yet come in. There's me, Thaddeus, Chester, and Owner. Oh, and I almost forgot, Old Ed was amongst us too, right beside me. I'm squeezed between him and Thaddeus, and Chester is on Old Ed's other side. He has some issues, Old Ed does. Anyhow it was mostly the same crew as usual, all of us running our mouth except Chester, who hardly ever talks unless you ast him a question direct. Usually he just looks blank at folks out of that peculiar white face like a Halloween mask or sits studying his beer like there's some sort of holy vision hid at the bottom of the glass and looking up at him. We warn't discussing anything in particular, so I says to Thaddeus, "If you could be anything, what would it be?"

"A liar," he said. "I'd be a liar."

Thaddeus says some weird things, but this sort of set me back on my heels, and I didn't answer right away. Then I said, "You're already a liar. Nobody tells big loose ones any better."

He said, "Not that kind of liar. I'd invent stories

about people that seem true, but actually they'd be imaginary. What writers do, and what you see at the movies."

"I don't get the point," I said. "Nobody believes them stories you tell anyhow."

"Neither do I," he said. "Anyway that's what I'd be, a liar."

"It's a testament, it surely is," I said. "What about you, Old Ed?" I said it to be neighborly. I never want a feller to feel excluded, although Old Ed has troubles of his own, and I doubt he much cares whether anybody notices him. One problem is that either he can't hear or he don't listen, meaning he probably don't care to listen even if he can hear, so I reckon they're the same. And he mutters to hisself so you're never sure what he says. As if this ain't enough, his brains is scrambled. The story I'm telling happened of a Friday night, and Friday nights can get rumbustious with the hollering and the jukebox and miners getting drunk and wanting to fight one another. Owner, he has his hands full of a Friday night.

Old Ed, he's famous in Scalded Creek, having outlived every doctor's prediction, and most of the doctors theirself. He'd been rolling on a disability from the mines for nobody knowed how long. What's he look like? Well, I'd describe Old Ed as a skeletal, thoughtful sort with black lung and psoriasis. His hair resembles combed dirt. While I was waiting for him to say something he turned around on his stool and spat a wet black object on the floor that looked ready to escape along its own slime trail. One time I seed him cough so hard he spat up a pink glob that looked like some spineless creature stranded out of water. It laid there on the floor quivering. Then he lit a cigarette and coughed up its twin.

Anyhow on this Friday night when he started talking it was to hisself as if I warn't even there, and it was me who done ast him the question. With all the noise the best I could make out went something like: "Suck out a sow's holler leg, old son. Prit'n near fail at everything. Why, you haven't got no chance of gathering in women that has a head start on you. Just scoot on down, righteous is what I'd call it. Think roadkill is canned ham, do you now? I kin see you, fool. Them raccoon eyes hungry after her. I ain't beside myself nor you, neither one. You think you seed us, but you ain't."

Don't expect me to explain what any of it meant. I have no earthly idea. Then I be goddamn if he don't slide off'n his stool and stand up, or stand as good as somebody in Old Ed's condition could hope for. It startled me, I have to say, and I give Thaddeus the elbow so he could look around and see too.

Old Ed started to yelling, "Sumbitch, I seed the thing head-high to Bald Mountain out yonder near four mile behind it. Warn't nothing anyone could have did. The thing would of took on King Kong and mashed him flat. So there I was, the snow ass-hole deep on a tall giraffe. . . " He paused to drop his cigarette butt on the floor and stomp it dead.

"Clean out of ammo when I heard the howl of the Abbagoochie. Things was froze solid all about, but when I heard that sound I begun to sweat grievous hard. They say the Abbagoochie don't eat nothing except full-growed wild-cats and maybe a wolf or two. It's well knowed they save the choicest morsels for the young and eat the bone and gristle theirself." He reached for his beer and took a swaller, but the effort had done wore him out. He climbed back on his stool and didn't make a peep the rest of the night.

Toward closing time he turned and watched Old Ed painfully dismount and move slowly to the door. He continued watching through the window as Old Ed leaned forward, the angle of his bend arrested by the swollen belly. He watched Old Ed pause near the edge of the weak porch light to put a forefinger against one nostril and blow snot out the other. After wiping the residue on a sleeve Old Ed stepped into a slow stagger toward the path up to the railroad bed and the waiting darkness.

He reminded himself that every mental represen-tation is merely a simulation, and for eidetic imagers there can be no barricade separating perception and imagination. Wait. What was that again? With sudden clarity he wondered who he was. It seemed absurd to think he had actually lost himself. You can't be lost and found in the same instant except in a quan-tum universe where such events are not considered peculiar. These thoughts seemed suddenly immediate and familiar. Could they be his own or had he heard them spoken by someone else a lifetime ago? Or were they only subliminal messages like those a dog captures when interpreting inflections in its master's voice? He glanced around. The bar, physically unaltered, had been transported to a different metaphysical plane. Jumbled thoughts and conversations out of time and context rode the air. He was aware he was drooling and took a paper napkin from the stack in front of him.

No one had noticed him listening to his personal voices like an eager ghost. In a rare moment he had felt another's dysfunction, and the monster stoking his own horror briefly unfolded its scaly wings and departed. The trace of a smile flicked across his ruined lips and quickly vanished like a dimple on a still pond after a dragonfly's foot touches down.

Scarecrow Man

The children called him Scarecrow Man, a name that he couldn't deny fit his description. The tissue damage that now defined him was irreparable and gruesome but at the same time wildly inventive. Who except a cruel and irritable god could conceive such a spectacle? He didn't mind; their taunts and gestures were harmless. They shared the same universe, an Appalachian hollow bisected by train tracks. Parallel to the tracks a black stream flowed like sinuous licorice toward an equally black river somewhere in a far valley. But the place where we stand is inevitably small. It must be to fit with human perspective. From his current location Vietnam seemed large and distant, but the places he stood over there—the jungle trails, the fields and paddies—had been constrained by edges. Each vista began and ended, just as here, just as everywhere.

What he couldn't forget was his pain. Once the physiological barrier between stimulus and response has been restored we remember the experience of pain but not pain itself. You can feel pain only at the instant of its delivery and never again recreate it in the mind afterward, unless it never goes away. In like manner you can remember the color blue, although the representational blue is only experienced in its immediacy. His pain had never left; its intensity had merely tapered off. Every surface nerve fiber shouted its agony through every minute of the day and night. Pain doesn't sleep. The new skin was tender and inferior to the original as if belonging in a deeper layer. Clothes were a constant source of hurt. If loose they shifted and rubbed; if tight they stayed in place but pressed persistently against him. He could never decide which situation was less objectionable. Direct sunlight and hot water? Anathema. He dreaded even the sizzling sound of his morning ham, backing away involuntarily when it popped in the skillet.

Doctors at the VA prescribed pain meds and called in renewable scrips he picked up on monthly bus trips to the drugstore in Mason. He read only the directions on the bottles, reluctant to learn the names of the drugs. They ameliorated his suffering some- what, but slowed his thinking, fused his memories, and jumbled the order of events both recent and past. Truth told, he was stoned all the time, the effect heightened when stoked by alcohol. If he acted as if under the influence it made no difference to the citizens of Scalded Creek because his entire pattern of behavior had always been attributed to the war wounds. His every flaw could be tacitly overlooked and thereby forgiven. It was God's will; a Job shuffles and totters among us. Of course he stumbles, they said to one another, he's got no toes. Sure he lurches when he walks. Burned up like that and in constant pain, wouldn't you? Have you ever looked into his eyes? No? Don't. They're disturbed.

Time lost relevance. There was day and there was night, separated by twilight. There was the constant noise from the tipple and the coal trains rumbling past. His own routine was now so ingrained that no concentration was necessary, a useful remnant of military training. In cold weather the first morning chore was shoveling out the stove ashes from overnight, carrying them outside in the ash bucket, and dumping them between the rails of the train tracks. Then he rebuilt the fire and brought in two buckets of coal from the bin. Following this he collected at least two buckets of coal from the sides of the tracks and emptied them into the bin, more if the weather was unusually cold.

Back indoors he swept and wet-mopped the floors and wiped down the tables, chairs, lamps, and kitchen counter with a damp cloth to remove the night's accumulation of coal dust. He showered afterward, made coffee, fed the dog, and fixed breakfast. After cleaning up and maybe doing a load of wash there was taking stock of food and dry goods and going to the store if necessary; regardless, he went to the spring to fetch a jug of water for drinking and cooking.

All this while semi-conscious, mind whirling numbly through archival memories becoming dimmer and more distant by the day. Once home he put on the two long-playing records he owned, one a collection by Master Desmond Casey that included "Danny Boy," the second by jazz saxophonist Ben Webster and featuring "Cotton Tail" and "Soul Time." Grady had ordered them for him. He didn't know why he picked either except the names of both musicians were stuck in a back pocket of unconscious memory and refused to slip away. Finally he could settle into his armchair and listen, getting up to lift the arm of the record player when a coal train approached and the shack started to quiver and shake.

His mind was mostly empty of abstract thoughts. Instead of narratives he snatched images and words from the air and tried frantically to piece them together. One notion kept reappearing partly formed, dancing tantalizingly behind his eyes then vanishing abruptly. It came more as a feeling of idyllic peace than a series of images, somewhat like a dream he was unable to restrain, identify, and describe. It had to do with an imaginary place devoid of tourists and lost specters where everyone is uniquely a native. Where the stones are compatible with your feet, each tree and flower distinctly different and found nowhere else. Everything from the color of the sky to the tiniest iridescent insect is recognized and known by name, and like the rocks and trees and insects the people share a commonality of spirit. Neither beauty nor ugliness exists, only sameness and the comfort brought by peace. There must certainly be such a place somewhere in the stretched reaches of the universe, a place beyond the shallowness and pain we know in this selfish world where nothing is valued just for itself alone.

Existence had become dreamlike. Now he heard voices in the daytime too. The voices made noises, but they never spoke, not really. Just gibberish mixed with laughter, cries, screams of pain. In the past he could understand what they said and even remember some associated faces, familiar gestures, a smile or frown, but no longer. Memories of a line of Marines snaking down a narrow muddy trail. Which was him? He must have been walking behind the others, maybe a tail-end Charlie because he could see only their backs, rucksacks bobbing up and down and rifles slung from shoulders. Four Marines waded across a paddy, tensing for an ambush, silhouettes backlit by late afternoon. Behind them the flattened sun, like a cracked egg, spilled its orange yolk across the horizon. How many? Think. Focus. He strained to see as they moved in and out of shadow, switching places. Was he one of the four or was he a fifth watching at a distance? Yet how could he simultaneously observe and participate? Was he ever one of them? Something in his memory had been juxtaposed; this was time out of time. He sat in his armchair and looked toward the tipple. Afternoon light reflecting back from the rain-spattered window revealed a pale ghost of his image, and in it his face seemed peppered with tears.

Thaddeus

Thaddeus had been watching Randi Sue carefully while salting his beer. When she left the bar area and went to the tables behind them, he said, "She's a poster girl for that famous saying, 'The way to a man's heart is through my vagina.'"

"Amen," said Thrice.

"Then," Thaddeus said, "you've got to ask yourself what rides shoulder-high to a wind-blown skirt?"

Thrice said, "I haven't got even a goddamn sniff of what you mean."

"Neither do I. It's something I just threw against the wall to see if it stuck. You know me well, gentlemen. I'm a tolerant sort, and I'm prepared to forgive her procreational proclivities, presumably perpetuated by ignorance and sloth and a certain whorishness that seems to run through her line. I once met a similar lady during my many travels. I recollect it was in Timbuktu. She's probably still there and at this very minute receiving a foot of muscular tongue from a dark knight of the alleys, a prince of the dust-flecked desert."

"Dammit, shut up, Thaddeus," Owner said. "You

never been farther away than Logan, and you're dis-respecting my only waitress. If she hears you and up and quits then you and Thrice will be tossing dinners off the arm while I set here holding a shotgun on your worthless asses."

Thaddeus turned to Thrice, "Time to change the subject. I believe we've pissed off the innkeeper. Do you recall your school days?'

"They're a dim memory."

"Well, so much for that proposed discussion."

Thrice said, "I'm told that over in 'Nam the stray dogs feed on the bodies of the dead, ain't that right, Danny Boy? He nodded, so I reckon it's true if he says so."

"It's only fair considering that country's citizens eat the dogs, and I could name a dozen reasons why," Thaddeus said.

"Don't try me," said Thrice.

Just then Randi Sue stretched and stood on one leg with her back to them so she could lean into the service window and shout an order at Bullis.

"My god, what a splendidly muscular leg!" Thaddeus said. "It reminds me of a snake ingesting something objecting strenuously to digestion." Randi Sue turned and glared at him. She was a smorgasbord of muscles and tendons, of pads of fat strategically placed and taut skin radiating heat.

"I see it as fiercely wanton when topping a high-heeled shoe," said Thrice. "Which reminds me. Do you recall a young couple that lived up the holler a year or so back, then moved away real quick? They had them a giant python for a pet and used to feed it live rabbits, big ones. As I recollect, Fish and Game come and took it away after it swallered their new-born baby silently in the night without even a belch, in its crib."

Thaddeus turned toward him. "Thrice, in all my days I've never come across someone who mistakes the barn door for the bull's ass as often as you. What we're discussing here is the reliability of narrative, whether the person telling a story is being truthful."

"We are? Hell, I thought we was talking about Randi Sue's legs. I must of missed something."

"We were, but then life moved on. Didn't I just say I can recall her as a teenager? She was lithe and long of leg even then, with burgeoning sweat-er-bumps poking out through her hopeful training bra. But we're now past that discussion, and you never noticed."

"You never said it."

"Well, I thought it, which ought to be good enough. You've just confirmed my theory that life is a conversation in which one party is deaf and the other dumber than hell, so I partly blame myself. I wish for a time of prosperity, I really do. We must discontinue this subject of sex. It's dangerous for men our age unless they're willing to give themselves over to the reckless torment of the young. Daily pussy leads to babies and responsibility, and you're way too old and ugly for either. The word *passion* comes from the Latin *passionem*, which means suffering, or enduring, as in the passion of the Christ. Get on out there and experiment with sex, if you dare. Go find a young one and make her muffin twitch. You'll sure as hell learn that passion isn't what you think it is.

"Now, I'm changing the subject back to narrative, so pay attention. I'd hate to lose you again. Suppose I tell a story and it goes like this. Picture me sitting naked on a commode in a crowded train station trying to read a newspaper while travelers trapped inside the transparent cylinders of themselves jostle and push against me on their way somewhere. Would you consider that to be a reliable story or a goddamn lie?"

"A lie, I reckon, but I'm having trouble getting that picture to stick."

"Right! That makes me an unreliable narrator. Now take Danny Boy's story. He's sitting right here beside me. He can't tell it to us because he's unable to speak. His dog can't relay it to us because he's a dog, even if Danny Boy could have told it to him. Anyway who would seriously believe a nameless dog? So what's left? I'll tell you. Danny Boy's story has become our own, and even though we don't know what actually happened to him it can't be—and never was—his. And your imagined version of it is different from mine, Owner's, Chester's, and Old Ed's, presuming Old Ed's ever thought about it. Point is, I'll bet we all believe it, even if it's never been repeated out loud. We humans are such suckers for stories, so convinced of their universal truth, that we want to believe them, provided the storyteller seems honest and tells his tale sincerely. So how does this work? We consider Danny Boy to be honest and reliable because he's our friend, then we tell his story to ourselves inside our separate heads and suddenly we're reliable narrators. To ourselves, at least."

Thaddeus took a swallow of beer and continued, "Every truth is a lie on some level, but some lies can still be truthful."

Thrice took a swallow of his own beer and looked thoughtful. "You blowed right by me on that one."

"Think of it like this," Thaddeus said. "Given a choice between a good story and the truth, most people choose the story. We know what happened to Danny Boy over in Vietnam, sort of. Something awful. Should we believe him? Take the Bible. The prophets told some real whoppers, but only a fool would think they're true. Nobody sets out seeking personal ruin and degradation, living on honey and grasshoppers and such unless he's freshly escaped from a nuthouse. Still, probably everyone in this camp believes in such shit, except me."

Thrice raised his glass and took a sip. "I take it you don't believe in the teachings of the church," he said.

Thaddeus said, "When have I ever said I did? Church teachings don't say a damn thing useful about real life decisions. For example, if confronted by a shaved pussy, supine and there for the licking, what would Jesus do?

"Preachers and other charlatans try to tell you it's all in the narrative, that the way of telling it—the language—can be bland and nobody would notice because it's the message that counts. But they got it ass-backwards. The truth is in the music, in the shakes and rattles, in the grimaces and grins and other face-tunes. In the farts and obscenities. My point? Every story is important, but how you tell it is what gives weight. And all stories are normal; it's us who are strange. You can't always be sure what's reliable and what isn't because stories get retold. They're laundered like old socks, then dried and used again. Don't try saying different. I've seen it and heard it.

"We have some evidence that on the surface Danny Boy is a reliable narrator despite not having spoken a word in our presence. But even if he isn't it doesn't make him a liar. Maybe he truly believes his memories, and if we can't prove otherwise then we have to take them as the truth. And we have to extend him the benefit of doubt especially if his memory is shot or even just confused.

"So what evidence do we have? First and foremost is his appearance. He obviously shouldered some serious distress over there in Vietnam. I mean, nobody comes home looking like him if everything went along right fine, wouldn't you agree?"

"Yep, there's no doubt that some terrible shit come down on him," Thrice said.

"And we know he saved a little money to buy a house, which is logical when you consider the circumstances. Where in hell could a man spend his money while he's lying half-dead in a hospital bed month after month, all expenses paid?

"And finally, we read his letters to Twyla Ray in which he described the typical situation out there in the jungle, not in great detail maybe, but near enough to prove it was dangerous as all hell. Through those letters we got to meet the other members of his fireteam. I recollect there was Poke from Texas who favored his horse and rifle over any human. Injun was a Seminole from the Everglades and an expert tracker. Bunny was a big black kid from New York and a botanist who had gone to college. Then there was the mysterious LT, the man he admired most, practically a father figure. The 'LT,' I presume, stands for lieutenant, whether first or second Danny Boy never said. Not that it matters, but we can ask." He turned to Danny Boy. "Was he a second lieutenant? No? Then he must have been a first lieutenant, right? Okay, a first lieutenant."

"I believe we're all thinking Danny Boy was the onliest one that lived through that experience," Thrice said. "But we don't know it for certain. In fact, we never ast him." He leaned around Thaddeus and looked at Danny Boy. "Was you the onliest survivor?"

He nodded.

"You sure?" said Thrice.

He nodded again.

"Did you see the others after they was killed?"

He shook his head.

"Then did they tell you they was all dead at the hospital?"

Again he nodded.

"Well, I reckon we have the answer," Thrice said.

Scarecrow Man

Is it possible to feel nostalgic for a place you've never been? Since coming to Scalded Creek he had been haunted by a vague feeling of displacement, as if he didn't belong. The people were friendly and obviously remembered him, but his memories of them seemed secondhand, as if gathered piecemeal from the scrap heap of his life before the war. He wondered if feeling alien among your own kind is normal. But then, he reminded himself, what is normal? Certainly not him, so he left it there and tried to forget what was evidently an inextricable situation.

The persistent tinnitus sometimes drowned the voices inside his head. They seemed to emanate from distant conspirators or old acquaintances, persons he somehow recognized from the war but was unable to associate with faces or events. They spoke not to him but to each other, using his mind as a sort of meeting hall from which he was excluded despite being the landlord. They came and went intermittently and uninvited during lulls in the tinnitus and carried on unintelligible conversations among themselves, reminiscent in their opaqueness of Old Ed's monologues. They forced aside his own thoughts as irrelevant or nonexistent, causing his head to ache fiercely and leading him to reach for the bottle of bourbon now a fixture beside the armchair.

Underneath everything was what the war had bequeathed: unexpected bouts of terror, flashbacks of explosions and blinding light followed by conflagration and howls and moans of the wounded and dying. Something as old as geology buried deep inside his being had become worn thin by the trivial shit of humankind and could no longer control its temper. On occasion it burst out of the ground pushing up trees and boulders with the intent of destroying the whole goddamn world. There was nothing he could do except hide somewhere else inside himself and hope to be spared.

False glory sold by recruiters praised the songs and battle cries spun into the ether, never mentioning the grunts and screams, the harsh poetry of war's devastating residue. More than anything, such abstract concepts were, for him, difficult to formulate and beyond articulation. Maybe they always had been. Either way, in their place he felt compressed physiological urges, primitive and more akin to pain, molecular mechanisms of suffering unlinked by any bridge to reasoning and comprehension. His needs and means of satisfying them had degenerated and belonged now to a lesser life-form. He recognized his devolving situation but could do nothing to reverse it. Had he ever been a reader, for instance? Maybe, although any confirming evidence was gone. He struggled to understand the menu at the Smokehouse Grill. Had he been formally educated? Was he once a purveyor of skills and knowledge? Why couldn't he recall? Perhaps he only imagined occupying a former life in surroundings different from these. He told himself to set aside half-formed thoughts and fleeting puffs of memory. Whatever the answer, it made no difference now.

He scarcely noticed the tipple after these many months, its sounds having gradually metamorphosed into background noise. The passing trains still triggered anxiety and fear, especially after dark when they approached bearing the shape and size of the night. Their proximity and weighty rumbling and the quaking of the shack were indistinguishable from incoming artillery shells. Their brilliant headlamps were the intensity of exploding white phosphorus, which he waited in terror to settle on him, anticipating the flesh dissolving from his bones. He slept fitfully, anticipating each approaching coal train and awakening fully before it reached him. Then he pulled the blankets over his head and curled into a trembling ball, fearing the impending heat and pain, afraid to see the flames licking up the walls and rushing toward him. At these moments he yearned to be anywhere except where he was. Then it was over except for the neuronal heat lightning flashing across his cortex, the residual kinesis of an organic object oscillating between life and death.

He was free to abandon the shack and move away, but to where? An impossible hidden valley littered with shards of ancient enlightenment and populated by singing prophets? Another coal camp in another hollow blanketed with smoke from a different slate dump and haunted by its own dystopian dreams in billowing sepia? How about a place without trains? In any case, what would actually change? He recognized at a liminal level that someone can disregard the continuous experience of living inside his body until it becomes so disfigured as to be nearly uninhabitable. Then he aches to abandon what remains, its ugliness and stink, and scrabble away like a hermit crab without a shell, naked and vulnerable.

A house, regardless of location, is merely a building. You can leave it and move elsewhere taking along your person—or what's left of it—intact. But the rooms of a damaged body are intersected by bleak corridors that echo with pained silence. The scaffolded walls, alive and innervated, are the color of sorrow. Escape is impossible because all exits have been sealed; misery and you are indivisible.

Where was the evidence that death ends suffering? It certainly isn't true for those who believe in the eternal fires of damnation. But he had seen those fires, felt himself singed by them. He had toppled into Hell's open mouth and never emerged. The hope that all will pass is an empty one. The hours persist, the months and years. You sleep and on awakening see that the clock's hands have not moved. How is it possible when only at the speed of light does time stand still?

Dreams are familiar images we can't recognize. For a week or so he had experienced flashes of what seemed like memories, but they were strange and disconnected, arising without warning and quickly vanishing, more like dreams retained into wakefulness. He skulked inside his rooms as if hiding in a corner of his personal shadow, trying to see clearly through this mental fog. In one, a photograph of a white hunter appeared. The man was smiling and holding a high-powered rifle while posing beside a slain rhinoceros, pith helmet shoved saucily back on his head. Where and when had he seen it? There were no clues to the hunter's identity, just a mysterious vacancy where context belonged.

Because it was Halloween he decided to get to the Smokehouse early. He could not recall from past Halloweens whether the place would be more crowded than usual, and he wanted to be sure of getting his stool. Already children were dashing back and forth across the tracks dressed as witches and ghosts and hobgoblins, pausing to stare before recognizing him and shouting, "Hi Mr. Scarecrow Man! Happy Halloween!"

By the time he arrived the last of the sunset was being consumed inside the infrared burn of its own rage; soon smog from the slate dump would be hurrying on the dusk. He and the dog limped down the path to the door. They were too early for opening time, but the door was unlocked. He saw chairs still piled on tables, their skinny chrome legs pointing at the ceiling like upside-down Rockettes. Owner and Randi Sue were bustling around, and Bullis was clanging pots and pans in the kitchen.

He slid onto his usual stool to the immediate left of the barber's chair, and Owner set down a glass of beer. "Bullis, he's been here since eleven making his soups and egg salad, and such, and his slaw, but it's still too early for supper." There wasn't anything to do, it seemed, but to await the night. And try to excavate those flickering disturbances in his mind.

Grief is a state of entropy in which fragments of memory disperse until equidistant from each other, at which time perspective narrows and we strive for closure. Except that truthfully there is none; the ends of the string never connect in a circle. What remains is only the gradual dissolving of images and sounds that once seemed alive.

He felt unremitting sadness for what he couldn't remember. He was already a wraith, an entity without presence. His destiny was even bleaker: a crumbling husk shuffling along the train tracks trailed by a crippled dog without a name. And underneath everything was a deep reservoir of guilt for the woman in the ville. Her death was his only specific memory of the war. Since regaining consciousness at the hospital he could clearly remember her shouts as she ran toward them brandishing the sickle, the echo of the rifle report off the mountainsides, the sight of her body contorting in a slow ballet of death, even the tiny tuft of earth dislodged by one of her feet as she pivoted away. What he could not recall was pulling the trigger. Why had that instant out of all the others been blocked from his mind when the rest of the event seemed so translucent? And the others, his fellow Marines, how had they been reduced now to shadows?

Their faces had returned on one occasion recently while he and the others were bellied up at the Smokehouse. Business was slow that evening, and Owner joined them with a beer in hand, leaning forward on his side of the bar. Thaddeus, Thrice, and Owner were discussing the letters he had written to Twyla Ray when Randi Sue walked past and mentioned she still had them. She said Twyla Ray had given them to her for no particular reason other than she was planning to run off, she thought, with Weasel and didn't want them anymore. It seems Danny Boy had been her backup plan. However he was across the world in a place she'd barely heard of and would never see, and Weasel was right here, which made her choice easy. After saying this Randi Sue had looked at him and shrugged.

She fetched her purse from underneath the bar and extracted a fistful of envelopes, six in all. Thaddeus arranged them chronologically by postmark, opened each in sequence, and read their contents aloud. Because Danny Boy's fireteam had never directly engaged the enemy the news was mostly about members of the team, their interests and personalities.

Listening to Thaddeus, he suddenly associated the names with faces, distinctive laughter, gestures, even locations. He could see partial images of cammies, hear muttered conversation, almost smell the fear as Injun claimed he could. There they were, all of them together, except the LT. Thaddeus was at the moment saying something about how the LT had just checked their feet for jungle rot and now they were standing around him in a loose half-circle as he gave his periodic talk about alertness in the bush. He saw himself, Hillbilly, slouching and looking down at the muddy ground, appearing the same as he might in a photograph; there was Injun, rain dripping in rivulets down his bare skin, hair long and black and twisted; Poke's lean, intense profile came clearly into focus, a damp cigarette hanging from his thin lips; and Bunny, looming above them all, listening dutifully to the LT although obviously distracted by the form or color of a nearby plant.

This improbable shift in consciousness was exhilarating, if oddly disquieting. Possibilities of redemption surged through his thoughts like a wild river, but his mind had been cosseted too long, perhaps as his brain was healing. Too many questions still awaited answers. Why was the LT a presence instead of an image like everyone else? Why did the LT's words seem to emerge from his own mouth instead of the LT's, yet it was clearly the LT who was speaking? And how could the perspective from which he could view himself be visible to others but denied to him, the seer? This juxtaposition of identities was startling. Yet there he stood barefoot in the mud affecting a characteristic pose, unaware it was one of his defining qualities, a part of what made him distinctly Hill-billy and no one else. He realized the impossibility of anyone observing himself through someone else. That unknown entity peering out through his eyes had been him, and without his even thinking about it had both created and defined the limits of his world. But the biggest question of all remained: who was he?

He couldn't stand to be there any longer and rose to leave. Owner said, "Hey, you ain't ate yet. I was just about to put in your order."

"We didn't mean to hurt your feelings none by reading them letters," said Thrice.

Only Thaddeus remained silent. He replaced the letters in their correct envelopes and stacked them on the bar. "Owner," he said, "I believe I'm in need of a refill. And I'd hold off on Danny Boy's order. He won't be coming back tonight."

By then he and the dog were already out the door and starting up the path. Whoever said the dark can't breathe? It can; I've heard it many times rasping hard against my cheek.

Owner

After Danny Boy and his dog got up and left all of a sudden the rest of us sort of stayed where we were not talking much. It was strange. Each of us knowed inside that sooner or later Thaddeus and Thrice would get into it good and things would be back to normal, so for some reason we waited. If there's one thing you can take to the bank it's them two causing a disruption. Seems all they got to do is show up and there's a disturbance trailing along behind like a beer fart. Tonight they come in as usual; that is, Thrice trying to shoehorn Thaddeus through the doorway in his chair and getting it stuck. As usual. And then Thaddeus starts cussing at him. As usual. Danny Boy and the dog was already here and in position to spend the evening, which warn't usual because they don't generally show up that early.

Anyhow because it's Halloween I thought I'd cheer the place up some. Randi Sue set little ceramic pumpkins with candles in them on all the tables, the kind of stuff I keep in the back and only bring out on special occasions. And her and me was wearing these pointy cardboard hats covered with sparkles. Soon as Thaddeus gets settled in his chair and pumps hisself up to bar height, I ast him how do I look

"Like a celestial fairy," he says. "Now skip over to the taps, Twinkle Toes, and draw Thrice and me a couple of cold ones before I asphyxiate your lame ass with pixie dust." That sets Randi Sue to laughing so hard I thought she'd wet herself. Thaddeus can be funny as hell sometimes, when he ain't being mean.

It looks to be a normal night except the kids showing up for trick or treat, then Randi Sue gives them candy I'd bought at the company store just for tonight. Usually their parents was along too, thinking they're cute by pestering me for a free drink as a treat. I laugh and say, I'll treat you real good, but it's going to take cash money. Then the rest of the regular customers trickles in and order up. The night is no bigger nor smaller than normal, despite being Halloween.

Danny Boy has a few beers. As usual. He's so quiet you'd never know he was even around if it warn't for his terrible appearance. Of course one reason he's quiet is because he can't talk. Got no voice at all. He can't tell you if he's happy or feeling puny. It's a damn shame, really, but I doubt even God could fix him. Not wounds that bad, they're permanent for sure.

Thaddeus had read them letters Randi Sue showed us, and then Danny Boy and the dog just up and leave. He don't pay me direct. He don't even carry money. Pockets is useless with them hands. It's a wonder he can dress hisself and halfway tie his shoes. When I said before I don't extend credit to nobody I'd forgot about Danny Boy, but with him I get paid regular as the sunrise. I keep a running tab and on the first of every month I go up to the company store where Grady looks over my arithmetic and pays me with Danny Boy's money he keeps in the safe. It's disability money from the gov'ment, although Grady's told me that there's still some savings. However Danny Boy don't need to touch it. His disability money takes care of his needs just fine. I ast why them savings ain't in the bank over at Mason gaining interest, but he says Danny Boy don't care about interest, that he'd rather leave his money at the store where he don't have to ride a bus somewheres to look at it. I reckon that makes sense.

Danny and the dog has long since went home, and it's near closing time when Chester busts through the door. I don't mean to say he busted *down* the door. Chester would never do that. He just opened it and busted in desperate, like his ass was afire. Chester never moves that fast, so us that's left looked at him in surprise.

Chester lives up Nigger Holler near to Bullis, my cook. He's a railroad engineer working second shift. Been doing it thirty years. How do I know? Because he reminds us often enough, like he ought to get some kind of service award. He pulls trains filled with new coal from our tipple to the train yards outside Logan where the line of cars is transferred to a long-haul engine drove by somebody else and tugged on along to a power plant at Detroit or Cleveland or the like, one of them big plants that eats coal by the trainload.

At the train yard he picks up another line of cars, these ones empty, and brings it on home where he positions it underneath the conveyor so's the cars can be filled up again and the train drove back to the train yard by his replacement driver. Back and forth, back and forth. When his shift is done he showers off, changes clothes, and either comes here or heads on home to the wife.

So there we sit, or if you're me and Randi Sue, there we stand, all of us looking at Chester. He rushes over and sets down at the bar and I immediately draw him a beer. "Fresh keg," I say. "You're in luck."

"My ass," he says. "If this be luck then I don't want none of it. God has done begrudged me any luck I had left. I been doing this same job thirty years. It's a good job, and I never regretted a minute of doing it until today. Just shows how things can change on you quick as spilled coffee."

"Thaddeus then pipes up and says, "Goddammit, Chester, what the hell are you jabbering on about? Your face is even whiter than usual."

"And you appear to be sweating fiercesome hard," Thrice says, "like you got a terrible case of the sorries."

"I just got done being interviewed by the constable," Chester says, and takes such a long swaller of beer he near drains the glass, like he's been stuck out in a desert somewhere. "'Nother," he says, and I oblige him.

"Our own Constable Bill?" says Thaddeus. "I didn't realize he spoke any known human language. Generally he grunts and scowls and scratches his balls to communicate."

Thrice looks at me direct and grins that stupid grin he has. "Wait for it," he says. I know exactly what he means. Thaddeus is feeling it now.

He says to Chester, "Do you know what the term 'constable' actually means? Well, I'll enlighten you. It comes from the Old French *conestable*, which in turn is from late Latin *comes stabuli* translated liberally as 'count, or head officer, of the stable.' In layman's terms, he supervises the shoveling of horseshit."

"Now that we got that settled," Thrice says, "Why not tell us why you're so riled up and out of sorts?"

"I thought you'd never ask," says Chester. "I'm pulling out of the tipple as usual, driving at the same rate I always do, which is about as slow as a coal train can roll and still be moving onward. And I'm blasting the whistle even more often than usual because it's Halloween and there's kids running back and forth over the tracks. If you think seeing the little bastards in daylight is hard, try nighttime when they're all wearing black costumes.

"So I've just pulled out of the tipple, like I say, and about to reach Danny Boy's place. Them boys operating the conveyer knows how to shove every bit of coal they can into a railroad car. When one car is loaded and I jerk the engine forward to position the next one the filled one looks like it has a black spine running down its length, the coal has been piled on so high. Of course, as I move along it gets shook down. My crew knows that when I get a little past Danny Boy's I tap the brakes a touch, just a little bump, enough to knock a goodly amount of coal practically onto his porch. It's my gift, considering he's been charitable and bought me beers and even supper a time or two when I come up short on occasion between paychecks. The nights is getting chilly, and I wanted to be sure there's plenty of coal he can pick up for winter. As y'all know, he don't move so quick, and picking coal must be a trial.

"So we done that, or rather I done it. I give the brakes a tiny tap to make the cars start a chain reaction of jarring one another at their couplings and sending a little shiver down the whole string. Out of habit I blowed the whistle a couple of licks, and suddenly right in my light I see a goddamn scarecrow with its arms extended like they make them, and a dog standing beside it. The first thing that come to mind was some fucking kids put it right there in the middle of the tracks to mess with me, knowing I couldn't stop in time so as to not hit it. Well, I did hit it, and I killed Danny Boy and his dog both. Neither of them flinched. They just stood there looking into the light, and my train run them over. I feel terrible, but I couldn't help it. I stopped soon as I could, but that takes a while, and of course by then it was way too late."

At that point Chester lays his head down on the

bar and starts to bawl like a calf, his whole body shaking. The rest of us don't say nothing for a long, long minute. Then Thaddeus, he says, "Well I'll be goddamn. I should have anticipated this happening, or something like it."

"Like Danny Boy killing hisself and his dog?" said Thrice.

"Exactly like that. If we accept certain assumptions to be true the outcome is completely logical."

"I'm glad you think so," I say.

"Chester, look at me," Thaddeus said. Thrice picked up his glass and leaned back so they could see one another direct. "It isn't you fault. There's nothing you could have done, so don't feel guilty. It was suicide by train, plain and simple, which our very own numbnuts Constable Bill must surely conclude, even if he otherwise doesn't have the sense to pour piss out of his own boot. Our companionable freak who occupied this stool beside me merely realized the truth about himself and didn't want to continue living. It happens."

Well, a few days go by. Danny Boy didn't have no living kin anybody knowed of, so there warn't a wake. His remains was real chewed up, as you might imagine. The dog was just a few bits of fur and bone, barely even roadkill. Grady paid the burial costs including the price of a marker out of Danny Boy's money. There wasn't a will so on Grady's recommendation his house and money went to the miner's fund to look after widows and orphans of them killed in the mines. They buried his remains beside the rest of his family, Remo and Glossy and Baby Beaver even though Thaddeus said then and still does it was a mistake.

A week goes by and everyone is gathered at the Smokehouse, as usual. Thaddeus comes around like a tornado at suppertime, same as usual, cussing at Thrice, who's trying to steer the wheelchair amongst the tables and up close to the bar. When the ruckus settles down and him and Thrice is holding alcohol, Thaddeus looks around the room. Present at the time is me and Randi Sue and Bullis back in the kitchen. Chester is there and Old Ed and a few others of the regulars, including the two miners who helped Danny Boy fix up his shack. Thaddeus tells me to fetch Bullis and bring him out so he can talk to us all. And when the room quietens down he says, "Okay, y'all listen up. That wasn't Danny Boy we covered with dirt last week."

"Then who the hell was it?" says Thrice, taking a step backwards from his spot at the bar, although he warn't no more nor less surprised than everybody else.

"It was the LT," said Thaddeus.

"Horseshit," I says.

"How many think it was Danny Boy? Raise your hands," Thaddeus says. A roomful of hands reaches for air.

"You see?" I say. "That was Danny Boy alright."

"You don't decide the truth by a vote," Thaddeus says. "I was just curious what everyone thought. Not that the LT would care. Far as we know he didn't have family, so where he's buried is irrelevant, both to him and to us. But think about this. All Danny Boy's letters were scribbled in the same hand. I don't doubt it was his writing. However the first parts of the letters read differently than what comes later. They're more, well, 'literary' in a sense. He admits in the fourth letter that the LT was helping him to compose his thoughts. I believe the LT wrote the first parts of those letters and Danny Boy then copied them and added what came later without consulting the LT. That's why he misspelled Mississippi and some other words more than once, and why his letters don't read clearly. So in my opinion Danny Boy was killed in that explosion over in Vietnam along with Poke, Injun, and Bunny. It was the LT who survived, and when his brain healed sufficiently some of his memories came back and suddenly he knew his true identity. The knowledge must have been overwhelmingly depressing. Anyhow that's what I think."

"Well, I don't believe it," Thrice said.

"Me neither," chimed in the rest of us together, almost like a choir. "That was Danny Boy," I said. "I knowed him since he was a baby, and there's not a doubt in my mind."

"Nor in mine," said Thrice.

I could see nodding heads all around. "Well, I truly don't give a rat's ass," said Thaddeus. "And I'd mean that sincerely even if I had a rat's ass to give." He told us we can all believe what we want, that according to the paltry data presently available death as an event matters only to the living. He said he don't like describing others and guessing who they might be because when we die we turn transparent in people's memories, and then they'll see him as I'm a liar, or worse, an inventor of souls, a painter of invisible images. He said he don't want to be any of them things.

Then Thrice pipes up and says, "You told me once you wanted to be a liar."

"And Thaddeus says, "I can't remember that. Was I holding alcohol at the time?"

"Matter of fact, you was," I recall Thrice saying.

"There you have it," says Thaddeus. "A man shouldn't be held responsible for what he says with a drink in his hand."

"Amen," I say. "And I'm buying drinks all around in Danny Boy's memory. And you don't have to accept one if you don't want, Thaddeus." I pull down a couple bottles of bourbon off'n the liquor shelf behind the bar and Randi Sue reaches to fetch a dozen or so glasses, one for each of us including herself. "A splash for everybody," I say, "in honor of our departed friend Danny Boy."

"Or whoever," I heard Old Ed say.

"Pour generously," said Thaddeus. "I'm a cultured man much given over to compromise, and it would be disgraceful to turn down a drink in Danny Boy's memory, wherever he lies. Two fingers at the least, and don't measure with the skinniest ones on your hand."

www.ingramcontent.com/pod-product-compliance
Lightning Source LLC
Chambersburg PA
CBHW021004260626
47169CB00006B/1937